The River Flows North

The River Flows North

A Novel

By

Graciela Limón

Arte Público Press
Houston, Texas

The River Flows North is made possible through grants from the City of Houston through the Houston Arts Alliance, and by the Exemplar Program, a program of Americans for the Arts in Collaboration with the LarsonAllen Public Services Group, funded by the Ford Foundation.

Recovering the past, creating the future

University of Houston
Arte Público Press
452 Cullen Performance Hall
Houston, Texas 77204-2004

Cover design by Mora Des!gn
Cover art by Dolores Orozco

Limón, Graciela.
　　The River Flows North: a Novel / by Graciela Limón.
　　　p.　cm.
　　ISBN: 978-1-55885-585-4 (alk. paper)
　　1. Immigrants—Fiction. 2. Border crossing—Fiction. 3. Voyages and travels—Fiction. 4. Sonoran Desert—Fiction. I. Title.
PS3562.I464R58 2009
813′.54—dc22

2008048577
CIP

9　0　1　2　3　4　5　6　7　8　　　　　10　9　8　7　6　5　4　3　2　1

ACKNOWLEDGMENTS

I'm grateful to many sources and colleagues for their assistance in the writing of *The River Flows North.* I thank the *Los Angeles Times* for its consistent coverage of issues related to immigration as well as the life experiences of those who risk all to reach our country. The reporters that I have followed have all been impressive in their coverage, and have been of inspiration for the novel: Sam Quinonez, Héctor Tobar, Daniel Hernández. I thank them all sincerely, and look forward to more extraordinary articles.

I most especially thank photojournalist John Annerino whose work, *Dead in Their Tracks* (Four Walls Eight Windows, 1999), moved and inspired me to write this novel.

I also thank those wonderful people who generously gave of their time to read first drafts of the novel: Roberto Robles, Herbert Medina and Mary Wilbur. My deep gratitude in this regard also goes to Stefanie Von Borstel, my literary agent, and Gabriela Baeza Ventura, my best editor.

I dedicate
The River Flows North
to my mother and father,
immigrants from Mexico,
who made it possible for their
children to achieve the Dream.
—G.L.

The narratives that follow are fiction inspired in part by true stories.

—G.L.

" . . . *la gran marcha* (in Los Angeles) . . . played out as a celebration of the essential dignity of being an immigrant in the modern United States."

Daniel Hernández
Los Angeles Times
25 March 2007

"It only made sense, then, that when he stunningly won an Olympic gold medal in freestyle wrestling, the Los Angeles-born son of undocumented Mexican immigrants (Henry Cejudo) would also share . . . his most beloved piece of cloth, the American flag."

Bill Plascheke
Los Angeles Times
20 August 2008
Summer Olympics, Beijing, China

ONE

Crossing to la Ocho

There is a pathway traveled by migrants that cuts away from the Mexican border as it slithers north through the Arizona desert up to Interstate 8. Migrants know this highway as *la Ocho*, the road that takes them to a better life, but the trail that leads to that highway is ruthless and unforgiving. Its sand, underpinned by sighs and shattered dreams, begins in Sonora, somewhere in *El Gran Desierto,* and slashes through Sonoyta on Mexico's side of the border. It swings in a westerly direction and crosses the line toward the American side at Tinajas Altas. At that point the route pushes north through the Lechuguilla Desert into Arizona and beyond, finally reaching *la Ocho*. There the pathway stops without reason or explanation. It just stops.

Hot wind blows through that desert corridor and sweeps across miles of sand; it swirls dust devils beyond the horizon, and its fiery tongue licks cactus and ironwood trees nearly to the ground. Only the craggy mountains that rise from the flat floor of the desert can withstand the blasts. They stand defiant, and even their names evoke fear: Gilas, Aguilas, Growlers and Mohawks.

From sunrise to sunset, saguaro cactus cling to the skirts of those mountains seeking shelter from the relentless sun. Like sentinels, arms stretched upward, they wait patiently for lost travelers to slink by, usually seeking the meager shade given off by their branches. And just as the saguaro cactus seek the shade of the mountains, other life holds fast to them. Slithery lizards creep in and out of crevices to avoid the dangerous rattler, and even the skittering scorpion. Plants and stunted trees jut out of cracked ancient rocks. Fearfully, they all await the inexorable sandstorm that will come as it has for millions of years.

Natives, *conquistadores,* settlers and prospectors have dared to undertake the desert crossing, and it is undeniable: The dead outnumber those who have lived to tell what happens on that passage. So many migrants vanish without a trace, although a bone or a skull or a mangled shoe is sometimes sighted. Most likely it will be an empty plastic jug that is seen skittering across the sand. Yet despite so much danger, human migrations go on. People attempt the crossing because they have dreams to pursue or oppressive lives to escape. Those people fix their eyes on Yuma, Dateland, Ligurta, Gila Bend and beyond. They change routes, crisscross and retrace their steps, because of the danger of being discovered by *la Migra,* uniformed men who drive unstoppable vehicles or worse, the others who call themselves vigilantes.

Despite the risks, some migrants make it to *la Ocho,* and once on that highway, the flow of people moves to where jobs wait. Word gets around when a letter with a few American dollars reaches towns in Mexico, in El Salvador or villages in Guatemala and Honduras. When news arrive telling that a loved one made it across, that he or she is at work in Pittsburg, Bangor or Hayward, then the many disappearances on the desert road fade from memory. It is at that moment that a tiny spark flares inside Demetria, Pablo, Braulio or Chela, until it becomes a bonfire. A few clothes are packed, and the cycle is set in motion, embraces are exchanged, and the perilous journey begins. Only words of warning linger: *¡Cuídate de la Migra! ¡Cuídate del coyote! ¡Cuídate del narcotraficante! ¡Cuídate . . . cuídate . . . !*

Most travelers are unsure where to go, but they head to dusty towns and truck stops like Sonoyta, el Saguaro, Los Vidrios, El Papalote, Ejido Cerdan and La Joyita. These places face Arizona on the Mexican side of the border. Rumors tell of shorter routes, less dangerous than others from where a man or a woman can walk the desert in two days at most, and finally reach *la Ocho*. Two days is not much, and it can be done. In fact, it's done everyday. All it takes is a little thirst and fatigue.

Soon men and women find themselves huddled together as they listen to a *coyote*. They don't know one another and refuse to reveal their names. They're too shy or too afraid. Instead, they eye one another to calculate age, and guess if that one is Mexican, Guatemalan or Salvadoran. Little by little, eyes take in shoes, or dress, or jacket, hoping to identify material or cut, and they look for anything that might inspire trust. Each one wants to know something about those strangers, but apprehension forces them to withdraw deep into themselves. Only later will they break that isolation and tell their names and stories. For the time being they are withdrawn and lonely. They turn their attention to the *coyote* and listen. Although they don't trust him, they must believe in him because they have to, he will be their guide. They agree to set out next day at dawn, following his lead through the desert.

The desert passage waits for the travelers. Some who travel it make it to *la Ocho,* then they head east and north to packinghouses in Kansas and construction sites in Illinois. Others end up in the beet fields of Colorado and the lettuce and strawberry harvests in California. But others stay behind with their dreams of the good life, and they haunt the pathway that might have taken them to *la Ocho.*

Two

Starting from La Joyita

Sonora, 2008

On a certain autumn morning, eighteen-wheelers rumbled off the road leading into La Joyita. Trucks, loaded with crates of tomatoes harvested from the fields of Sonora were westbound on the Mexican highway heading toward San Luis Rio Colorado. Others rolled in the opposite direction, empty after having unloaded their cargos. Whatever their destinations, the drivers were tired and needed a break.

The vehicles lumbered into the parking area of the truck stop. Clouds of yellow dust churned in every direction and showered people, clothes, walls and windows with white powder that shimmered in the dry air. On the fringes of the truck stop a cluster of silent migrants milled around, knapsacks strapped to their backs, and money pouches tied to their bellies. They waited patiently for *el coyote*.

The migrants knew what to expect. He would set the time to begin the trek, how they would make the crossing and how much he would get paid for his service, maybe half the price now and the full amount later. Although fearful, the travelers were ready to go through the last steps of their odyssey and launch out to the desert.

Leonardo Cerda, *el coyote,* was a scrawny man with skinny legs and barely of medium height. His mahogany-colored skin was cracked by exposure to the desert sun, and his eyes were small and slanted; they looked out from behind high cheekbones with the caginess of a wolf. As they stared at him, the migrants found it difficult to tell from his clothing if he was *tejano* or *mexicano*. His trousers were worn-out denim, and his cowboy shirt was faded with some of its pearl buttons missing. His sombrero was made of sturdy straw, but now it was shabby; its brim was soiled with layers of sweaty stains. His boots were almost new and cut in the cowboy way.

When he spoke, a lisp drew attention to the gap left by missing upper teeth. Chain-smoking had yellowed his lips up to his pencil-thin moustache, and a cigarette dangled from that toothless hole. He spoke a mix of Spanish and English laced with obscenities. His words were muffled or sometimes garbled. The migrants had to listen carefully so that they could fill in the parts they did not understand.

"*¡Órale!* Why's everybody just looking at me? We all know what we're here for, so don't lose time staring at me like you're a bunch of *idiotas*. My name's Leonardo Cerda. You can call me Cerda, I'll guide you to *la Ocho*. After that you're on your own. From there you can head to the east or to the west. I don't want to know where you're from or where you're going. I don't expect to hear anything about you except your *pinche* name. Okay! Let's get started. You, there, give me your name."

Cerda wagged a yellowed finger in the direction of a young man with tight curly hair. He appeared to be seventeen or eighteen years old and stood with hands pushed deep into his trouser pockets. He was slight of build and nervously shifted his feet from one side to the other.

"Sí, Señor. My name is Néstor Osuna, but everyone calls me Borrego." When the group giggled at his nickname, the young man joined in and goodheartedly laughed, looking around, nodding his head as if acknowledging some kind of celebrity. His face brightened, happy that his nickname had caused those morose-looking people to smile.

Cerda broke in on the laughter. "¡Borrego! Why do people call you that? *¡Qué pendejada!*"

"No, Señor, it's not stupid. It's because of my hair. It's so curly everybody says that I look like a sheep."

More laughter, this time hearty, making the group lighter, less afraid. Cerda took time to measure Borrego while he lit another cigarette from the stub that dangled from his lips. He cracked what looked like a smile. "Well, that's your business if that's what you want us to call you. Who's that standing next to you?"

"This is my brother."

"Does he have a name?"

Borrego's brother looked older, nineteen or so, and he glanced around at the group, betraying a deep shyness as his pale skin became tinged with pink. Unlike Borrego's hair, his was straight. He wore a tattered baseball cap, and what showed of his hair hung limp around his ears. He was taller than Borrego and thin like his brother. His shoulder bones stuck out of the faded pullover sweater he wore. He took a timid half step forward. "Nicanor Osuna, *a sus órdenes,* Señor."

Cerda glared at the young man and snorted. He looked away and took a long drag from the cigarette, obviously making time while he thought of what to say. "Okay, Nicanor. Let's see how long you'll be at my orders. You're skinny, so is your brother. How in the hell do you think you're going to make it through that *chingado* desert? Will you obey me when I say let's go, or will you cry for your *mamacita?*"

"We'll last, Señor." Nicanor's voice was steady. "We'll obey. Our mother is dead, so her spirit will be our guide through the desert, not you."

Cerda did not miss the sarcasm in Nicanor's voice. He even heard the difference when he spoke of his mother. The two men glared at one another until Cerda shifted his eyes while he pretended to dig around in his pockets for another cigarette. He was burning time because he was not finished with Nicanor. "Where are you guys from?"

"I thought you said you didn't want to know."

"*Bueno,* I just changed my mind. Where are you guys from?"

"Zacatecas."

"That's a big state. From what shitty town are you?

"Tecolotes."

"*¡Mierda!* Sounds like a witch town."

"No, Cerda, we don't have witches, just hard-working people."

"Okay, okay! Who's next?"

A young woman spoke up. She appeared to be in her mid thirties, of medium height and slim build. Her hair was chestnut colored and pulled back in a thick braid that reached nearly to her waist. Her face was oval-shaped, its skin olive-toned and her eyes were gray-green. Her most attractive feature was her nose, which was finely chiseled, giving her an aquiline profile. Cerda took time to ogle her while he savored her prominent breasts. He did this until she spoke.

"My name is Celia Vega."

Cerda said nothing as he gawked at the woman with his wolf eyes, and then he shifted his eyes from her breasts to her feet. He took in her sturdy shoes, her denim trousers and black jersey shirt. He wanted to talk more with her because he found her tantalizing, unlike the rest of that ragged bunch. Maybe later on, he told himself. His mind lingered on that thought for a while, but after a few moments he reluctantly shifted his gaze from Celia Vega to the man who stood next to her.

Again Cerda took his time to stare at the migrant who was obviously at least seventy years old. The elderly man was small, and he wore a threadbare jacket that nearly covered his faded overalls; it reached below his knees. His shoes were heavy but almost worn out, and he grasped a boy by the hand. The child was about ten years old, and he clung to the older man, almost hidden behind him.

"What's next?" Cerda blurted out. "Now I'm supposed to take an old goat and a baby across the desert! Shit! What's going on here?"

"Señor Cerda, you have no right to be disrespectful. My grandson and I will pay. You have no reason to speak that way. My name is Julio Escalante and this is Manuelito. We're only going halfway and then we'll come back to our *pueblo* in Nuevo León."

9

"Only halfway?" Cerda sounded scornful. "What are you talking about? Nobody goes halfway across that *cochino* desert and returns. You think we're going on a picnic?"

"No, Señor, I don't think that. We'll pay the full price."

"Don't expect me to lead you back!"

"No, Señor Cerda. I'm not expecting that."

Cerda yanked out another smoke to light from the one already crunched between his fingers. He mumbled and kicked at the sand, obviously disgusted. After a while, however, he appeared to accept Julio Escalante's plan, and moved on to the next person. "Who's next?"

A short, hefty woman in her early forties sucked in a deep breath and raised her hand while she stood in a way that expressed confidence. Her face was round; deep scars spoiled its dark skin as did a broken nose, but her eyes were filled with a mix of gentleness and strength. Everything on her was worn out. The long-sleeved pullover, which was too small for her, outlined strong shoulders and breasts. She wore faded trousers that were also too short, and her sneakers showed they had once been white but were now a dirty brown. Mismatched socks peeked out from between her shoes and the cuff of her pants; one had slid beyond sight under her heel.

Cerda tried to make her out so he eyed her with a slow, shifty look. His cunning told him that the woman was strong, the type that was a leader, someone who would not eat up his words like the others. She could be trouble, his guts told him. He had experience with her kind, except that people of her sort were usually male. "And you? What's your name?

"Menda Fuentes."

"Menda? What kind of stupid name is that? I never heard that one before. You sure it's not *mensa*?"

Cerda smugly looked around, certain that he would get a good laugh out of the play on words, but nothing happened. Instead Nicanor glared at him and Julio shook his head in disapproval. The others looked away in silence.

"No, Cerda, my name doesn't mean stupid. It's short for Imelda. My name's Imelda Fuentes. If you remember that much, I won't forget that your name is Cerda, not *cerdo*." This time the group laughed. The woman had outfoxed the fox, and they loved it. Cerda snorted, admitting to himself that his name did come close to meaning pig. He had been teased about it since he was a boy.

Everyone turned to stare at him as they wiped laughter tears out of their eyes, and they wondered what he would say. Before he spoke he remembered that he was not the only *coyote* around; they knew it, and Cerda knew that they knew it. He glared at the woman, and for once, the cigarette stub dropped from his lips without an instant replacement. "Okay, okay, I won't forget. Where are you from, Menda Fuentes?"

"I'm from Chalatenango in El Salvador."

Cerda glared at her while he started another cigarette. "Goddamn!" He cursed under his breath, and then his eyes slid over to a man that looked at him with a smirk stamped on his face. This one stood out from the rest. His posture and dress spoke of a different class, a different beginning. He was tall and light-skinned. His chestnut-colored hair was wavy and hung down to the collar of his shirt. His hands and fingernails were clean, almost manicured, and that was obvious when he put a cigarette to his lips. A ring he wore on the small finger of his left hand accentuated his sleek hands. All

11

the while Cerda looked hard at the man while he tried to make out his age. Maybe thirty, he thought.

The man had stood unnoticed on the fringe of the group, but when Cerda glared at him, all eyes turned to stare. Everyone saw that he was unusual. He wore a suit matted with fine dust. He held the jacket slung over his right arm and his shirt, sweat-stained around the armpits and collar, was of dark silk. His necktie hung unknotted around his neck. His shoes were wingtipped and seemed almost new, and unlike the others, this man did not have a backpack. Instead a long canvas bag rested on the ground wedged between his legs.

"Well, Amigo, are you on the way to the airport?" Fed up and irritated by his exchanges with the others, Cerda's sarcasm was heavier now. He was not going to be fooled or intimidated by the fancy clothes. By now Cerda had a cigarette stuck in his lips, and he fumbled in his pockets looking for a match.

"No, Amigo, it's not the airport for me this time." The man replied in a steady voice. "I'm going on the same picnic these people are taking. Your job is to get me to *la Ocho*. The rest is my business."

The man took a long drag from his cigarette as he stared at Cerda who, for a fleeting moment, thought he glimpsed a trace of nervousness, maybe apprehension, in the man's eyes. Cerda was on the verge of coming out with another wisecrack, but something warned him to go easy, so he decided to leave the man alone. About to move on to the last of the group, he remembered he had forgotten to ask the man's name. "What's your name?"

"Armando Guerrero."

Cerda felt tired, and he did not want to say much more, so he turned his wolf eyes to the tiny woman standing by

The River Flows North

Guerrero's side. She was old, maybe pushing eighty, but she was sinewy, and she looked tough. Her thin gray hair was pulled back in a tight braid that emphasized her high cheekbones as well as her small narrow eyes reminiscent of an ancient Asian mask. The white cotton dress she wore reached her ankles, and although its embroidered fringes were soiled, it was still beautiful. She wore only a rebozo around her shoulders.

Cerda looked at her and knew that she was from the far south, somewhere down in Mexico or maybe Guatemala. He wrinkled his brow as he stared at the worn-out *huaraches* that barely covered the woman's bony feet. "Abuela, do you think you're going to make it across that *chingón* desert?"

"Señor Cerda, I don't want to make it to the other side."

"No? Then what the devil are you doing here?"

"I'm going to stay with the spirits of my ancestors." The old woman's voice was steady and clear. "I'm not going to *la Ocho*, nor am I returning. That's why I've come."

"The spirits? Don't tell me you're one of those *locas* that believe in that shit?"

The old woman did not respond to Cerda; she only looked at him, a stubborn expression stamped on her face. He stared back at her while he thought of her heavy indigenous accent. He had come across others of her sort, people who believed in spirits. He paused to think back to his youth and the old town healer, Doña Milagros, *la curandera*, who had almost snatched his brother from death with her rubdowns and potions.

He scratched his scraggly chin and secretly admitted that maybe he did believe that the desert was haunted and that the old women knew what she was talking about. Who could count the hundreds of fools that had perished out there in

13

that inferno? And where else would those ghosts go? They probably just stuck around the desert pathways moaning, sighing and scaring the hell out of the live ones. He even admitted that he had heard strange sounds more than once on his desert crossings. Cerda dropped the subject. "What's your name, Abuela?"

"Encarnación Padilla."

"Where are you from?"

"From very far away." Doña Encarnación said no more.

"Okay, let's get down to business. Here's what I'm gonna do for all of you. I'll take you through the passage I know best. It's not the shortest, but it's not the longest. It's pretty safe from patrols and the other son of a bitches that hunt down people like you. The trip will last three nights and three days. Take at least two gallons of water for each day, more if you can carry it. Even the kid and the old lady will need that much, so some of you will have to help out. We'll need more water when we use up what we take, but I know a water hole close to the end. Take only dry food that's not heavy, something like tortillas or jerky. You'll have to pay half right here and the rest when we reach *la Ocho*.

"If you're serious about the crossing, come over by that truck to talk to me. If you don't like me, there's more than one *coyote* standing around. Look over there." Heads whipped around to look at two parked vans. "They're empty and waiting for people like you. Those *ratas* will promise to take you across the river into Texas, and then drive you through the desert to Houston. Just like that." Cerda snapped his fingers. "But what those son of a bitches don't tell you is that besides you, fifteen or twenty or more *cabrones* will be stuffed into those moving coffins. And it's *adiós mamacitas* and *papacitos*."

14

The River Flows North

Eyes widened and then became slits filled with suspicion; they had heard what he was talking about, so they believed him. When Cerda had barely finished what he said, a barrage of questions slammed into him. He swiveled his head first in one direction and then in the other, trying to make out who was saying what, but their voices blurred.

"Why so long, Cerda? My buddy did it in two days and two nights!"

"Where's the border? How'll we know when we've crossed to the other side?"

"How many kilometers to *la Ocho*?"

"Where can I get water and food?"

Cerda shouted back trying to block the flurry of questions. "*¡Órale!* Not so fast! Calm down! Give me a chance! First, it's about seventy kilometers from here to *la Ocho*. I know that you think that's not too long, but it's not like walking from one *pueblo* to another back wherever you're from. Here it's all sand, and the heat will slow us down real bad during the day. We can't walk at night because that's when the snakes come out. Some people try to do it, but I know of too many dreamers who died that way. Those rattlers bite real hard and their poison works so fast that a body gets all bloated until it blows up in a matter of minutes. So I'm not taking any chances. We'll walk only when the sun rises until it sets. Doing it that way takes about three days and nights. What else?"

Nicanor asked, "Where's the border?"

"Over there, on the other side of the road." Cerda pointed. "See where there's only sand? Right there is a dry arroyo. That's the line. When we cross it tomorrow morning you're there, almost where the gringos live." The migrants stood on tiptoe, stretching their necks, pivoting heads, squinting eyes and trying desperately to make out the magic line. Beyond it the dream waited.

Cerda went on. "Behind the café is a shed that has everything in case you don't have what you need. *Bueno,* I'm going to the truck and wait for those of you that decide to come with me. I'll tell you right now that I'll be here tomorrow at four in the morning to lead you. If you're here, you're here. If not, *adiós,* amigos!"

The migrants grumbled at what he said. Each one looked around and then down at the dirt searching for the answer to the apprehension they felt deep in their bellies. Most had traveled hundreds of miles to reach this point, yet there was hesitation because of unanswered questions.

It was Celia who first broke the ice and spoke to the group as Cerda left. "Maybe we ought to think it over. I mean, what's going to happen once we're out in the middle of the desert?"

Nicanor tried to answer Celia, but he only hit on another fear the others felt. "*Bueno,* that's what we came for and if we stick together, we'll be safe. That doesn't scare me as much as when I wonder what it's like over there where the desert ends. What if there isn't any work?"

Borrego answered his brother. "That's not the worst part. First comes *la Migra.* Everybody knows that those guys grab you by the neck and throw you out just like you're a starving dog or something worse. And what about Cerda? What's to keep him from cheating us? What if he's lying about the water holes? What if he doesn't know what he's doing? Or worse, what if he's a traitor? Everybody knows that some *coyotes* sell out to bandits."

These questions only set the rest of the group on edge because on top of so many doubts and fears, they all felt shaky even about one another. They eyed each other with suspicion. They knew nothing except each other's name, and even that could be fake. How could anybody in the group be trusted? Maybe they were criminals, *narcos* or worse. Everyone back home warned against that type of monster.

As the minutes passed, their fears and agitation grew, especially because they were aware that Cerda kept glancing at his watch every few seconds. They looked at each other, hoping to discern the truth stamped on faces, but they only found eyes that stared back with a blank, jittery expression.

Menda Fuentes was the first to make her way toward Cerda, and they saw that she moved with confidence. When she walked over to the guide, something relaxed inside them and filled each one with relief. They watched as the woman and the man haggled. She gestured and pointed toward the desert, wagged her head in disagreement; she kept quiet while Cerda counted on his fingers. She kept silent as she gazed out at the desert as if measuring, figuring, putting things together in her mind.

After a while, the group saw that she nodded in agreement. While the others watched her, she reached deep into her bra, pulled out a pouch, counted and handed over what everyone saw were bills. The deal was struck. After that, even without knowing just how much Menda Fuentes had paid, one after the other they followed her lead.

THREE

Menda Fuentes

*M*y life began when I saw my mamá, papá and little sister murdered along with hundreds of other
people at el Río Sumpul as we tried to escape
into Honduras. It was 1980, and I was sixteen
years old. It also was the beginning of the war, a time when
rebels and government soldiers fought like dogs while they
tore at each other's throats. Both sides said they fought for
justice, but all they did was destroy our villages and kill those
caught in the middle. The war went on year after year. It dev-
astated El Salvador from top to bottom, leaving behind a trail
of death, misery and countless broken women left to care for
fatherless babies.

There were other tragedies and massacres, but whenever I
think of that war I think only of the day at Sumpul when I
was a witness to the slaughter of innocents. There were so
many dead that the river became clogged with bodies of chil-

dren, women and men. We didn't know it, but government soldiers were waiting to block us from crossing the river. Killing us was easy for them because they had machine guns and rifles, even helicopters that came at us from above like giant flying scorpions. We had nothing.

Among the victims was my baby sister who was hit by several bullets all at once. I saw when her little body was torn out of my mamá's arms. It happened so fast that my mother didn't feel when it happened. I tried to reach mamá, but it was impossible because I was pressed underwater and carried downriver by the many bodies. When I was able to push myself above water, mamá and papá had disappeared. I screamed out for them, but the explosions of machine-gun fire and the roar of the flying scorpions drowned out my voice.

I wanted to die so I stood erect, very still, and waited for a bullet to liberate me, but nothing happened. Waves of terrified people dragged me toward the edge of the river until we were on the other side in Honduras where the crowd made its way to a village called Mesa Grande. When we marched through those streets, people stared at us because they didn't understand what was happening, but after a short time we were treated with kindness.

I remember that I was lost, cold and hungry as I moved from one cluster of people to another, begging for morsels of food and drink. I answered questions that might tell people who I was and where I was going. I was disoriented, alone. It wasn't until a woman, Doña Altagracia, came to take me to stay in her house that I regained a sense of reality.

I stayed in Honduras and lived with that good woman while I worked at whatever I could: sometimes it was in the fields, other times it was cleaning houses or sweeping streets.

Whatever money I made I gave her, and she was satisfied. I can't say that I remember clearly what my life was like at that time, probably because I was in deep shock. Pictures of that terrible day at the Sumpul robbed me of sleep, and I barely ate anything until I became skinny and hunched over. Those were hard times for me, but Doña Altagracia brought me back to health, and after a long time, I recovered my strength. My heart was broken because I lost my family. My thoughts were filled with them and my uncles and aunts still living in El Salvador, but no matter how much I tried I couldn't find anyone to put me in touch with them. As days and months passed I convinced myself that they, too, must have been killed.

It wasn't long after that I met Jacinto Morales, the man who became my husband. I met him on a Sunday as I left Mass when he happened to open the door for me to step out to the street. He smiled and looked into my eyes as if he had known me for a long time, and I returned his look. That glance turned out to be an invitation for him to follow me down the street, across the plaza and even to the door of Doña Altagracia's house. From that time onward we were hardly ever apart. I liked him because he made me forget everything, especially the anguish of seeing my parents and little sister murdered. In a short time, I thought I loved him.

Jacinto was twenty years old. He was handsome, cheerful and polite, and what astonished everyone was that he didn't smoke or drink. In a town filled with drunkards, Jacinto stood out. Whenever he visited, he would bring me a small bunch of flowers or maybe even a chocolate, but it was with Doña Altagracia that he showed the most consideration. He managed to speak to her of matters that interested her, although no one understood how he knew what she liked. It wasn't long before Doña Altagracia told me he was the son she never had. He didn't talk of war or politics, and this was something people admired in him because those were times when whole families were torn apart when they discussed governments and insurrections. Jacinto seemed to sense what each person wanted, and he always said the right thing. All along, I fell more in love with him.

I knew that tongues wagged and tried to discover his faults, but all they saw was that he made a good living as a young carpenter, and in that small town where everyone knew everything, the town gossips had to admit that he would be good for any girl. Those old women looked at me with little smiles and eyes that twinkled while they rubbed their wrinkled hands imagining what was going to happen between Jacinto and me.

I wasn't yet seventeen when he asked me to marry him and without much thought I accepted. It was a mistake because that was when the real Jacinto peeled off his mask, and although it didn't happen all at once, when it did happen he never changed. For a long time I blamed myself because of what occurred on that first night after the wedding. The truth is that I was a shy girl who didn't know what to expect, so when he got near me I told him to leave. He looked angry, but then he laughed and said he could wait.

I was grateful that he left me, although he returned in a while. This time he acted like someone I didn't know. Without explanation he became rough and hostile. At first I thought he was playing until he took my arms and twisted them painfully. I screamed and begged him to stop, but he laughed. After that he got on top of me and forced himself between my legs. He hurt me so much that when he was fin-ished I managed to run away, but that did no good because he followed. When he caught me, he pushed and punched me in the stomach and shoulders so hard that the pain nearly made me faint.

After that night I discovered that there were two Jacintos: the one everyone saw and the other one that pushed, slapped and pinched me when no one looked. I don't know why he assaulted me that way. I wondered why he married me in the first place; when I asked him, he laughed and said he married me because I was beautiful. I knew that he mocked me because I'm not beautiful. During the years that followed hardly a day passed that he didn't tell me that I was stupid, that I was fat and too short, that I was a prieta, because my skin was so dark and that I looked more like a monkey than a woman. The insults were endless, and they hurt me even more than his pounding fists. When I told him how much his words offended me he did it even more, and he laughed until tears squeezed out of his eyes.

This torment went on every night, even when I tried to please him by giving him everything he wanted and by pretending to be happy to see him despite the deep repugnance that grew inside me each day. I tried to convince myself that it would end, that he would change, but as time passed I saw that he enjoyed hitting me and offending me. The more I tried to do things his way, the more he attacked me. The time came when I didn't dare look into his eyes because I discovered that this gave him the signal to begin the assault. I saw, too, that he always made sure not to hit my face, always striking me only where the bruises hid under my clothes. And along with his fists came the threat: If you ever leave me, remember that I'll find you and kill you!

Although the secret Jacinto came out during nights when we were alone, that didn't mean that I was free during the day. His favorite torment, even when we were with others, was to pinch me in the soft underside of my arms, right near the armpit. Only someone who has been pinched that way knows how much it hurts, and he did it while he pretended to help me cross the street, or when he made others think he held my arm as we knelt in church. It hurt me so much that although I didn't cry out, tears rolled down my cheeks, and people wondered what had happened.

I thought of leaving him often, I even planned it. But I was afraid that he would follow and kill me. I was a coward. It took years for me to overcome that fear, but that was only when the pain got bigger than my dread. On that day, I ran to Doña Altagracia to beg her to let me live with her again. She allowed it, but only for a few days because my place was by my husband's side. When I blurted out the truth of how he tormented me, she cried a little, but, after she wiped her eyes, she told me that every woman has a God-given cross and that, in time, Jacinto would change. I listened to her words and a few days later when Jacinto came to the door, I allowed him to take me by the arm back to his house.

Not long after I had a son, a child that looked like me. His face was so sad because he knew how miserable I was. Throughout my pregnancy he had heard me cry and beg Jacinto to stop the assaults. The little boy didn't last. He died a few months before he reached his first birthday. I know that it was pure sadness that took him.

I lost several babies after him. How could they live when their father beat me almost every night? In my anguish, I couldn't explain how it was that Jacinto planted his seed inside me only to beat it out with so much cruelty. Eventually I managed to have a girl and then another boy. I'm convinced that they came into this world only by miracle.

As the years passed, Jacinto became more confident; now he battered my face as well as the rest of my body. He no longer cared what anybody said. But all things end, and the day came when I finally knew that I would not take more abuse. I can't explain what came over me or why it took so long for me to change. Perhaps it was my children and how much they suffered all those times that they saw my bleeding, swollen face. Or maybe it was the same instinct that pulled me out of el Río Sumpul when I felt ready to die. Whatever it was that transformed me, it has not left me. From that time, I knew that I would never again suffer Jacinto's attacks, never again would I allow him to hit me, even if I risked being hunted down and murdered by him.

People must have seen the change in my eyes because they asked me what I was planning to do. I didn't take a moment to answer that since God had sent me that cross, I had decided to send it back to Him. I was finished with it and with whatever else God had in mind for me. I know that my words scandalized the women around me, but by now I didn't care. It was my face, my body and my soul, even my children, that were on the verge of being wiped out, and I wasn't going to allow it!

On the day I made up my mind, I walked out the door of Jacinto's little house with nothing else except what I was wearing, and I kept moving toward el Sumpul. I walked without stopping. I don't remember how long it took, but when I got to it, I plunged into the river not caring if it swept me away or drowned me smashing me against rocks. What I did know was that never again was I going to tolerate that stinking jackal's cruelty.

Burning in my heart were constant thoughts of my children because I knew that I had abandoned them. I didn't for-

get that I was leaving them without a mother, but they were now old enough to take care of themselves. I knew also that I was the one Jacinto hated. His beatings had worsened with time, and I knew that sooner or later he was going to kill me. Then what? Wouldn't my children be left without a mother when that happened? With me gone, at least my absence would keep them from seeing their mother murdered. Leaving my children was a terrible decision for me, but I had no choice except to live or die, and I chose to live. I hoped this would give me a chance to join them later on in a more human life.

I retraced my steps back to El Salvador, and I didn't stop until I reached Chalatenango where I wandered up and down streets. I hardly recognized anything. Everyone was a stranger to me. Thoughts of my mamá and papá flooded me just like they had when they first died, and I thought only of my little sister who would now be a big girl, more or less fifteen years old. I wondered about my family, my uncles, aunts and even their children. Where were they now? Maybe they were all dead. I couldn't be sure because I hadn't heard from them.

The war had just ended, but its marks were everywhere. There were broken-down houses with missing walls; whatever was left of structures was burned and charred. Streets were filled with holes blown out by bombs; backstreets and alleyways were littered with trash or skeletons of burnt cars. I looked around hoping to recognize someone, but what I saw were gray, emaciated faces, their eyes dull, without expression. I was even more shaken when I saw people, even children, missing legs or arms. I realized that in my own misery back in Mesa Grande, I had forgotten about the anguish of others, that the snarling dogs of war had ripped apart *whatever crossed their way, and it had happened so close to me, just across el Río Sumpul.*

I made my way to the plaza where I sat under a twisted, sickly tree. I needed time to put together my thoughts because it occurred to me that I had escaped Jacinto's rages, but at the same time I had blindly plunged into another dark world, and I had done it without thinking, without planning, with nothing to keep me alive. Looming in front of me was the thought that I was alone. On the other hand, I reminded myself that I was alive, that there had to be a reason for my having escaped and that I had to keep moving forward.

Afterward, as I walked around the plaza, I was attracted to the church because I saw a crowd of women gathered in the courtyard. I became curious and asked what was happening. It turned out that the priest in charge was looking for a cook. Right away I was interested because I cooked, and I needed work, so I made my way through the chattering women until I finally faced Padre Ignacio. I had to look hard before I saw him because he's a short man, smaller than me, and the women milling around him blocked him from my view. What first caught my eye was the red bandanna he wore around his neck, just like a campesino.

When I got near, he signaled me to come to the front of the crowd. I saw that he looked intently at my face, probably recognizing the marks that told of so many beatings; maybe that was why he gave me preference over the other women. Something inside me made me feel relief, but I tried not to think of that because I knew that I didn't deserve any preference since I was the one who allowed Jacinto to have his way in the first place.

I started working right away and stayed for years while our town recovered from the scars of war. It was good because along with the job I got a room with a bed and a place to bathe. Those years were quiet ones, and what I liked most of all was that I felt safe, although I was lonely most of the time. This part was my fault because I didn't want to talk much to anybody so I usually kept to myself, except when it came to Padre Ignacio. Eventually, I confided in him, revealing my past life and why I had abandoned my husband and children.

Whenever we spoke about my life, he asked me questions without judging me; he never said that I was wrong. His only advice was that I had to be on my guard because Jacinto was sure to come looking for me some day. I knew that his words of caution were wise, and there was hardly a time when I didn't glance over my shoulder to see who was standing behind me.

My life was solitary, but it was at the same time peaceful. I missed my children, but praying for their safety helped me through each day, and in time I was able to make contact with Doña Altagracia who kept me informed about them. It turned out that Jacinto looked after them, making everyone think of him as a perfect father.

One day Padre Ignacio proposed that we set up an outdoor kitchen in the church's courtyard because there were people that usually lingered in the atrium after a rosary or a novena every night, but there was nothing for them to eat or drink. What better than a few benches and tables where those parishioners could enjoy a snack and beverage? I could be in charge and make extra pay and even get help to do the job. I agreed after a while.

We shook hands. With that I got to work staking out a space right there in the church atrium, and although cooking for crowds was hard work, I liked it because it took my mind away from the bitterness of my past life. At the same time it provided me with money to save. I wasn't sure what I was saving for until the day when my life again took a turn.

One summer night I was busy putting out orders, and, as usual, gossiping, laughing people surrounded me. Some were sitting on my benches, and others were just standing around passing time. The portals of the church were open to allow parishioners to walk in and out, some with rosaries clutched in their hands. There were shouting, playful children everywhere. In the midst of that commotion, I happened to glance up from the stove and my eye caught the silhouette of a man standing on the edge of the crowd. At first I didn't know what it was that attracted me to look at that person in particular, so I wiped sweat from my eyes to better focus, and it was then that I recognized him. It wasn't a mistake. The way he stood with his head tilted to one side, legs arrogantly planted on the concrete, thumbs pressed into his belt—all of it told me that it was Jacinto. My nightmare had returned.

In that instant I felt my head spin, blocking out everything around me, but my confusion passed as soon as I reminded myself that what I had expected for years was happening, and I had to face it. The thought flashed through my mind that friendly people would surround me if I let out just one yell. Yet, I decided not to involve anyone. I kept on stirring and flipping the orders cooking on the stove.

Nothing happened, at least not right away. Hours passed; all the time I kept waiting, never losing sight of Jacinto. Out of the corner of my eye I watched him when he slithered across the courtyard, far away from me, where he squatted on his haunches against a wall, sure that I couldn't see him.

28

The River Flows North

Although darkness covered him, the glow off the tip of cigarette after cigarette gave him away.

The night came to a close, and our parishioners drifted away; it was closing time so my help rolled the stove and pans into the usual shed. As that was happening, I put an iron skillet aside, leaving it close by. I can't say what I was thinking. I just did it. Finally, my workers wiped tabletops, swept up scraps of food missed by stray dogs, took off their aprons, and said goodnight. I knew that I still had a chance to ask somebody to stay to keep me company, but I didn't. Although I was afraid I wanted to confront Jacinto once and for all, and I had to do it by myself.

I was alone. I stood without moving, my ears wide open expecting a small sound, something that might signal that he was there next to me. The courtyard was silent and almost in darkness except for the overhead lights illuminating the church's entrance and walls. Minutes dragged by and there was nothing, not even the crunch of boots on leftover food, or the heavy breathing I remembered so vividly, but after a while he appeared out of the gloom, and he stood glaring at me with his mouth clamped shut. All along his body said that he felt confident, strong and even powerful; that I was nothing but a worm.

What followed was violent, but it was the last time because I had already made up my mind that never again would I put up with his meanness. When I married Jacinto I was less than seventeen and my thinking was that of a little girl; that made it easy for him to abuse me. As the years passed, my thoughts became different, clearer, and my mind was now that of a grown woman who knew that he had no right to treat me with cruelty. So I faced him as never before, *and I glared into his eyes, waiting for him to make the first move.*

When he sprang at me I was ready, but I didn't move fast enough to avoid the blow; he slapped me with the back of his hand so hard that it sent me reeling backward, making me lose my balance. I fell, but when I got back on my feet, I came up with the skillet clutched tight. At that instant I took a swing that came down on him with all the force in my arm. He wasn't expecting the iron weapon when it crashed against the side of his face, crunching bones in his ear and jaw.

He didn't have time to whimper because he lost consciousness even before he thumped flat on the concrete. When I saw that he was knocked out, I put the skillet back in its place along with the other pots and pans; then I wiped my hands on my apron. Without looking back, I went to my room where I bathed and went to bed.

As if drugged, I fell into a deep sleep. I don't know how long it was before shouting and someone pounding on the door awakened me, screaming for me to leave the room. I didn't think of dressing or anything. I just ran out barefooted and in my nightshirt, but the shock of the sight of flames wrapped around what had been my food counter stopped me. Close to me people were running back and forth with buckets filled with water, and I saw Padre Ignacio pulling a garden hose that was letting off a puny stream of water.

I joined the fight with a blanket that I yanked from my bed, trying to snuff out the edges of the fire, all the time forgetting that my feet were getting burned. We were all trying desperately to put down the fire, but it was useless; the blaze was too big and we had so little to fight it. It was a long time before the fire truck came with long hoses, but by that time what had been my tables, benches and cooking things were either melted down or just a pile of ashes.

When it was over I squatted on the ground to watch the smoking cinders, and I cried like I had not done in years, not since Jacinto used to beat me senseless. I wept because I understood that he had uttered the last word. The flames that destroyed my livelihood were nothing less than his hardest, cruelest blow.

I don't know how long it was before I felt someone sitting next to me. When I looked around I saw that it was Padre Ignacio. His hands and face were blackened by smoke and dirt, but he was not hurt; he was more concerned about my feet that were covered with red blotches. He shook his head as he handed me the red bandanna he yanked off his neck while he pointed a shaky finger at my feet. We didn't have to speak because we both knew who was responsible, and that the next time it would be my life that would be destroyed.

Padre Ignacio and I met the next morning, and he laid out a plan that I agreed to follow, but only after days and nights of thought. He told me of a church in the capital of the United States where women like me are given sanctuary. He explained that the people in charge there see to it that documents are drawn up for asylum if it can be proven that a woman's life back home is in danger, either because of war or something just as bad.

I listened to him, but it took me days to decide what I was about to do because I wasn't sure of the plan. I needed time to think it over. Truthfully, I was afraid to take such a risk by myself, and just as fearful of a foreign country where I didn't understand the language, where I didn't know anyone. Over and over I thought of how I would be a stranger walking unfamiliar streets and places. And what about the crossing?

Everyone knew how dangerous it was to pass through that border without documents. The more I thought, the more I wondered why any government would offer sanctuary to a foreigner who came empty-handed. What did they have to gain? It occurred to me also that such help would cost money, and I had very little. And most important of all, I asked myself what made me different from all the women in the world who faced husbands like Jacinto?

I hesitated for days while I forced myself to face so many fears and doubts. I told myself that it would be easier for me to run away to Honduras or Guatemala or even Mexico, but then I remembered that Jacinto would only follow. All he had to do was get the money for bus fares, and that was cheap. Only one thing would stop him, and that would be the border into the United States because that was the one thing he wouldn't dare cross. Jacinto was a coward. And then, when I was about to make up my mind to run away to the United States, I remembered my children. Would I ever see them again if I left my country?

My mind went in circles until these thoughts nearly over-whelmed me, so I turned to Padre Ignacio. He listened to me patiently, but I knew that he, too, shared my uncertainties. Finally, he helped calm my fears when he reminded me that I didn't have a choice, and he was right. The only thing left for me was certain death at the hands of Jacinto, because if he missed the first time he wouldn't fail the next time, and that without a doubt would leave my children without a mother. On the other hand, if I migrated al norte, in time I could send for them.

I collected my small savings, packed what I needed most, and with Padre Ignacio's blessing I rode a bus that took me first to Honduras, then to Guatemala, and from there across the border into Mexico. That journey opened my eyes and taught me that there were many of us doing the same thing. Oh, each one of us had different reasons, but at the bottom of it all, it was to escape intolerable lives. Bus and train stations were clogged with people, all of us with stories that told of bitter reasons for taking such a risk, especially for leaving homes and family.

I found highways crowded with travelers that asked for rides, even for a short distance, because it was important to save money. Sometimes trucks stopped, but most of the time drivers just honked and passed us up. Sometimes I thought that we were like a strong wind that blew in one direction: al norte.

When I crossed over from Guatemala into Mexico, I discovered that in that country la Migra is unforgiving with outsiders. Many of the officials are thieves; they take whatever they can from those of us from the outside. Others make a habit of violating women, and they beat men just to get whatever they think is useful. I don't know why we're so hated by some mexicanos. I can't find the reason, because, like us, so many of them are on the same path. We look the same, and we talk the same, yet there's something in those of us who come from outside of Mexico that betrays us, and it turns some of its people hostile.

It took me a long time to make my way up through Mexico. I did it on buses and old trucks. I walked for miles as long as it got me closer to the border. I ate what I needed to keep me strong enough to move, and I got new shoes only when the old ones fell apart. It was hard, but after I asked people where to go and kept my ears peeled to hear rumors that flew from one mouth to the other, I headed north through Sonora where I finally reached La Joyita.

Once there I moved from group to group while I looked, listened and asked questions. I saw some people get on trucks, but I saw others shake their head and move away from those vehicles as if they were afraid. It was then that I saw Leonardo Cerda talking to a few people, and something told me that he was el coyote to follow.

FOUR

Day One

The sun was about to rise when the tiny group followed Leonardo Cerda north across the dry bed that marks the border between Mexico and the United States. They did not know it, but they were heading straight into the Lechugilla Desert. Cerda planned to follow the path that hugs the skirt of the Gila Mountains until it snakes into the passage between its lower hills and mountains. After that, his target was Ligurta, which would put his group well on *la Ocho*. The hike covered thirty-five miles, and he figured that taking the journey over three one-day treks would be safe. He had done it many times before.

When daylight broke, the mountains that loomed to the right surprised Cerda's followers, especially when the high craggy ridges edged by the rising sun cast a shadow over them. The immensity of those mountains and the darkness created by them caused each one to feel insignificant and afraid. They looked around and realized that they, too, cast shadows, but they were only tiny specks against the sandy landscape. Everything that surrounded them was empty and foreboding, only here and there a saguaro cactus cast its long finger-like image on the surface, a silent sentry warning intruders of unknown dangers. To the north the horizon shimmered like an unbroken thread.

They kept no particular formation as they moved. For a while they walked in pairs, side-by-side. At other times they formed a single file behind Cerda, and they walked in silence with only a few words muttered from time to time. Their pace was measured, not too fast, not too slow, because they understood that saving energy was important. Don Julio held Manuelito by the hand, and in the rear were the Osuna brothers who already helped Doña Encarnación Padilla as she walked between them. The mountains protected them from the heat of the sun until the angry disk showed itself in full force when heat penetrated the migrants' thin garments. Those with hats pulled them as far down as possible as they tried to protect brows, necks and ears. Those without hats peeled off sweaters or yanked out handkerchiefs to wrap around their heads. The click of water jug tops sounded more often as they drank of the precious liquid until Cerda's loud voice shattered the rhythm of their pace.

"Hey! Easy on the water! We have a long way to go. No more drinking until I say so. One jug has to last you until tomorrow morning. Keep moving. Anybody that has to piss or anything else, do it fast and catch up. We'll keep on the move for another two hours before we rest."

Surprised eyes looked around to see if the others felt the same intense fatigue, but no one said anything, although each one inwardly thought that two hours was too long a time. The weight of backpacks grew with each minute, as did the thought of water in their jugs. Almost constantly, faces turned upward as if to beg the sun to stop its relentless rush to the center of the sky because they saw that each moment increased its rage.

Suddenly Don Julio stopped for a moment to hold his grandson against his body and shield him from the glare of the sun. "Cerda, Manuelito needs to take a drink. I'll give him mine." The boy clung to his grandfather and hid his face under the folds of the old coat.

"¡*Mierda!*" Cerda mumbled just loud enough for Don Julio to overhear. "This is what happens when you have brats with you! The next one to start bellyaching will be the old bag, right? Okay! Okay! Give the little shit a drink, but we've got to keep walking."

The migrants' eyes riveted on *el coyote,* then unspoken resentment crossed back and forth as they looked at one another. Cerda, on the other hand, was unmoved, but he did notice the sudden relief that came over them with that brief halt. The moment it took Don Julio to yank the top off the jug to allow the boy to swallow was quick, but feet that grew heavier by the minute welcomed the pause as if it had been a gift.

The heat soared, yet the march went on for hours. Each man and woman was locked deep inside of memories that transported them back to *ranchitos*, city streets, bedrooms, huts, family gatherings, laughter and tears. Thoughts swirled in the dry desert air and brought to life tender conversations as well as bitter arguments followed by kisses, caresses. Their memories were filled with lovers, and friends, some forgotten and some always remembered. The truth was that each head swarmed with sorrow blurred with hope.

Menda lifted one heavy foot after the other and wondered how it was that her life had become so intolerable that
it brought her to this unknown destiny. She did not realize
that Borrego, who walked by her side, inwardly asked himself nearly the same thing: What craziness brought him and
his brother down the hellish path they now walked?
Unknown to Menda and Borrego, the rest of the group had
the same questions. For all of them, the answer to so much
uncertainty waited up there on the edge of the desert where
the asphalt thread called *la Ocho* was ready to take them to
steady jobs and the good life. Life would be hard for a time,
they told themselves, but nothing like this intolerable hell.
Instead there would be shelter, maybe a little house, and soon
a family.

"*Bueno,* here's our spot. We can rest and take a few shots
of water. Eat something, but little by little." Cerda pointed to
a small clump of ironwood trees where the travelers collapsed. The branches of those trees, deformed by constant
blasts of wind, gave off blotches of puny shade. Too exhausted to speak, the migrants sprawled on the sand, covered their
faces with whatever hat or shirt they had at hand, and hardly remembered to reach for a tortilla or string of jerky; the
only sound was the swirl of water anxiously sucked out of
jugs. Cerda eyed all of them, but focused on the two older
ones as well as the boy. He saw that they appeared to be
keeping up.

He sat on his haunches, took a sip of water and lit up a
smoke from the stub dangling off his lips. His wolf eyes quietly scanned the horizon and then glared at Armando Guerrero from under the brim of his hat. Although he had come
to terms with him back at La Joyita, he was still jittery about
the man. Cerda eyed the long canvas bag and tried to guess

what was in it. When he finished his cigarette, he lit another one and got to his feet. He knew where they would spend the night, and he had to get the group going so that they would make it before sunset. He shoved his backpack onto his shoulders and barked out the order. "*¡Vámonos!* And watch out for snakes!"

As if weighed down by lead, the migrants first shifted, then sat up, and soon they were on their feet. No one grumbled, only deep sighs cut through the arid air. They fell into a single file, but more than one of them thought that they heard sighs and soft moaning that came from under the sand, even from behind the gnarled trees they had left behind. No one said it, but they were afraid.

Well into the last part of the trek, the group halted abruptly at the sight of what was evidently a burial place where rocks spelled out the name *Olga;* at its side there was a small cross. They all stood absorbed and frightened; no one spoke as they listened to what sounded like sighs carried by the wind that swept down the gloomy mountains. They wordlessly eyed one another, convinced that what they heard was real. The moment was shattered when Doña Encarnación spoke, her voice dry and brittle. "No one knows how many bones are buried under this sand. Which one of us can imagine how many souls linger here, still waiting to reach their dream?"

Her words caught everyone by surprise, especially because she had hardly uttered a word since the beginning. Even when some of them grumbled and others complained, she kept quiet, so now as she spoke, their heads snapped in her direction as if yanked by a single thread, eyes wide with fright.

Cerda caught on to the migrant's apprehension right away, and he stepped in to block it. "Okay, okay, everybody, that's enough. I don't want you to get nervous. These things happen all the time around here. Dead people are all over the place. We don't see their bodies because the sand covers them up pretty quick. This one was lucky. She had somebody to put these rocks up to tell us she's here, but the wind and sand will take care of business pretty quick. When the next *compañeros* come around, nothing will be sticking up out of the sand."

The migrants stared at the stones as they moved away and stepped cautiously as if trying to avoid invisible dead bodies. No one said anything because their hearts beat so hard that words could not come out of their mouth. They had heard rumors of people who died in the middle of the desert, but no one had expected to see anything like it so soon on the trek.

Suddenly Doña Encarnación spoke, "I saw her."

"What do you mean?" Cerda was growing tired of the old woman.

"I saw the spirit of the poor woman who is buried here. She walked ahead of us for a long time, waved her arm and told us to follow her. She doesn't want us to die. Look at her. She's standing over there."

Faces swung in the direction the old woman pointed at, but they saw nothing except a glare off the sand. Cerda was about to spit out another vulgarity, but something held him back. She was an elder, and he had already treated her with enough disrespect, but even more important, who knew if she really did not see the phantom? Besides, he had walked these places with other migrants who swore that they saw the walking dead. He pushed his hat down to cover his eyes as he mumbled under his breath.

"*¡Mierda!* Maybe I'll be one of those goddamn spirits even before I know it."

Without another word he waved the travelers forward with an outstretched arm and again began the trek. They followed him, but he could tell that they whispered behind his back. He knew they were mumbling about the ghost; that the only reason they did not see it was because they did not try hard enough. When he abruptly turned to face them, the murmurs stopped. Although they put on expressions of innocence, he knew they were exchanging doubts, fears and maybe more stories about other spirits, the ones back home.

After that brief pause they walked on while the heat soared to an intensity that no one except Cerda thought possible. Their clothes were soaked with sweat, and their ears, noses and faces became caked with sand. They tried to spit out sand that sifted into their mouths but this was almost impossible as their tongues became dryer. Their feet felt like bricks, and breathing became more painful with each step. Soon pieces of clothing were shed and flung to the side of the path. As they trekked, none of them could forget Olga, left behind in her makeshift grave, and they imagined how painful her death must have been. Without admitting it, each one looked in every direction; they squinted their eyes expecting to see the woman's spirit pointing the way to safety.

The sun began to set when Cerda pointed to a cluster of large boulders that stuck out of the sand and formed a small shelter. He waved everyone forward to let them know that the place was their overnight protection. Without any questions, backpacks were dumped as each one of the migrants gratefully dropped on the sand, some with their backs against the side of the rocks, and the others flat on the ground with legs stretched out limp and crooked.

"Not so fast, Amigos!" Cerda was quick to interrupt the break. "We have to put together a fire so the coyotes won't feel like eating us. See all around us? There're lots of sticks and roots and other pieces of wood that we can burn. Okay, everybody! On your feet! If we shake our asses we can get a fire going. We need enough to last the night. C'mon!"

A loud drawn-out groan escaped as the group fanned out to gather fuel. Nobody spoke, but they kept an eye on the landmark boulders so they would not get disoriented. When they regrouped, it was Cerda who fixed the kindling and struck up a fire while he barked out a few words. "Just relax! Eat a little bit but drink even less. You can sleep. I'll wake you at dawn so we can hit the passage again. You're doing real good, so I think we'll reach Ligurta when I said we would."

Each one found a spot around the fire, some sprawled out, but most of them sat up while they ate or took furtive sips of water. Manuelito wiggled under his grandfather's arm and fell asleep immediately. Doña Encarnación sat alert with her back straight and legs crossed; her small slanted eyes glinted with the reflection from the fire while the rest hid behind a blank expression, wrapped in private silence. The wind's soft moan and the oncoming steely light of a nearly full moon masked the apprehensions each one felt.

After a while, Nicanor pulled out a harmonica from his shirt pocket. The instrument was hand-sized and battered, and when he put it to his mouth, soft music spiraled through the smoky night. What he played was melancholy, lilting, and everyone turned to look at him; even Cerda gawked at him with interest. The campfire cast images on those sad faces, but soon Nicanor's gentle music captivated them and forced tiny smiles and little crinkles around their eyes that had been sorrowful minutes before.

Then a voice began to sing, surprising everyone even more; it was Borrego who sang along with his brother's harmonica. His voice was light, pure, rising and falling like water cascading over pebbles. Now all attention was on him, and they saw that in the light of the fire he was beautiful. His eyes were bright and his bushy, curly hair wrapped itself around his head like a dark halo. To his companions, Borrego looked like a brown angel.

Alma mía,
qué lejos de mi casa estoy,
pero por causa buena me voy.
Pronto llegaré al otro lado,
y allí encontraré mi destino.
Alma mía, alma mía, no me abandones
mientras busco mi destino.

The lyrics were short, catchy and the others felt good enough about the song to join in, first humming, and then singing along. Borrego encouraged them to sing louder, to keep him company while he sang about his soul that would be a guide to the destiny waiting him. Encouraged, Nicanor played on with more assurance, and soon every one swayed, sang and smiled. Those that had been flat on their backs sat up to join the others. When the song ended, they yelled and clapped. Hands pressed against each other's arms, and there was backslapping, all of it with joy. They wanted more music.

Then Borrego jumped to his feet as Nicanor pelted out a *corrido norteño*. He danced around the fire, stomped his legs, swung his arms in the air and wiggled his butt back and forth so much that the others broke out with loud laughs, their mouths wide open. He mimicked a dancing couple. He whirled and held his invisible partner by the waist while he romped, jumped and swayed until he got his *compañeros* to shout for more.

¡Ándale, Borrego! ¡Dale duro! ¡Más meneo!

Then, all at once, they jumped up and danced without shyness or stiffness. Even Cerda joined in, and his skinny legs jiggled in midair to the rhythm of the *corrido*. Nicanor did not miss a beat on his harmonica as he danced. Manuelito mimicked the grown-ups and shimmied his shoulders while he kicked his feet as high as he could while he followed the beat. The only one that kept apart in the shadows was the well-dressed stranger. He reclined against his canvas bag and watched what was going on through half-shut eyelids while he took long drags from his cigarette.

Doña Encarnación and Don Julio did not stay out of the fun either. Exposing bony knees, the old woman shyly lifted her long dress so that she could move with more ease. She moved one foot first, and then the other, and kept with the beat. Don Julio went higher on his toes with each step and held his arms as if to embrace a partner. The two *viejos* danced, their movements serene, slow and more rhythmic than that of the others.

The rest of the group spun around the fire, arms outstretched over their heads, and they forgot that just minutes before they had felt so tired they thought they would die. On and on, they danced in rhythm, their long, gyrating shadows reflected on the still hot sand. As they danced, deep wells locked inside of them opened up and allowed fear, doubt, sadness and confusion to swirl and spike upward, to escape toward the immensity of the star-filled desert sky.

The River Flows North

Nicanor, finally exhausted, stopped playing, and everyone dropped back on the sand. Panting and laughing, they shed tears of relief because the ice that separated them had shattered. No one could explain why, but they knew it had happened.

"Okay, we better get to sleep. We have another big day tomorrow, and we need to be rested." Cerda jolted the group back to why they were in the middle of the desert. They all knew that he was right, but they wanted more of what they had experienced. They wanted to know about one another, and it was Don Julio who spoke. "I want to hear your names again and where you're from, and where you're going."

The migrants looked at each other understanding that this was a good idea, but who would be first? All eyes turned to Borrego, the brown angel. He laughed lightheartedly, his eyes even brighter now than before. "*Bueno,* you know that I'm called Borrego. My brother Nicanor and I are from Zacatecas. We're farmers so we're heading to the big farms in California." Borrego turned to his brother who nodded to let everyone know that he did not have more to add to what his younger brother had said. Still, no one spoke because they thought that he would say something else. When he kept silent, another voice took a turn.

"I'm Menda Fuentes, and I'm from El Salvador. I've traveled a long time to get here, and what I really want to do is to make my way to the capital of this country so I can get my papers and stay forever." When Menda stopped, she heard soft whistles and murmurs. She knew that they wondered what made her think that she was different from the countless others; why should she be given documents when others had to live hidden lives. She guessed their thoughts, but she was not going to say more. She had said enough. Besides, she had reached the desert; after that nothing was impossible for her.

Another voice piped in. "I'm Celia Vega from Venta Prieta. I'm not sure where I'm going but I had to leave my *pueblo,* my little girl and my husband because there's no work there and like everybody else, we have to eat." They all stared at Celia and felt sorry that she was forced to leave her daughter. More important, they wondered why she had left her family to work instead of her husband.

Doña Encarnación was next. "I'm from the Lacandón jungle, so far south in Mexico that it's close to where Menda Fuentes comes from. I'm of the Tzetzal tribe, and as I told you yesterday, I've come to stay in this desert. I want to join my ancestors." Low murmurs followed the old woman's words. Some felt a shiver come over them because they remembered that she was the only one who had seen the spirit of the dead woman Olga. They wanted to know more, but no one spoke up. Instead they looked at the quiet man, the one who did not dance.

"Armando Guerrero. The rest is my business."

There were sarcastic chuckles at the man's arrogant response because he only confirmed what they had thought of him from the beginning. They were convinced that he was a bigheaded opportunist who took advantage of their company to make it into the United States. Everyone lost interest in him and turned to Don Julio who had started the conversation.

"I'm Julio Escalante and this is my grandson Manuelito. We're from Torreón and we've come looking for my daughter, Manuelito's mother. When we find her, we're going to take her back home."

46

Cerda voiced what everyone thought. "Old man, where do you think you're going to find her? What city or town are you heading for? This is real big country, you know."

Don Julio answered, "We're not going to a city. I already told you yesterday that we're only coming halfway because here is where she died, in this big desert. Didn't she, Manuelito?" The boy nodded in response to his grandfather's question while eyes stared, trying to make sense of what the old man said. Even Cerda forgot to light a new cigarette.

"She died out here, in the middle of all this sand, and you're looking for her? What do you expect to find? Her bones? Her clothes? What are you looking for?" Cerda's voice was a mix of disbelief and frustration. Don Julio nodded, but he did not say which of the questions he was answering. A long sigh broke out from everyone, but Cerda had more questions.

"When did she die?"

"Months ago."

"How do you know she died? Maybe she's in some city right now, cleaning houses, or something like that."

"I know because Manuelito was with her. He saw her die. Isn't that so, *hijo*?"

Again the boy nodded and this time it was Menda Fuentes who broke into the conversation. "*Muchacho,* if you were with your mother and she died, how come you're still alive?"

Don Julio did not give the boy a chance to respond; instead, he spoke up. "Because Manuelito wandered for days in this desert, lost and thirsty, when gringos of a *Migra* patrol found him. They drove him back to Sonoyta, and from there someone called to let us know the boy was alive. I traveled by bus to pick him up. We went home, but after a while I decided to come back to find her. True, Manuelito?" Again the boy nodded.

Cerda shook a cigarette out of a bent pack. "Don Julio, are you crazy? There can't be anything left of your daughter. The *pinche* desert swallows up a body like it does a small lizard or a splinter of wood. Anyhow, how do you know what direction she took?"

"Manuelito remembers. We're sure we'll find something. Maybe some of her clothes, or maybe her bones are still out there."

"Okay!" Don Julio's stubbornness was too much for Cerda. "Everybody go to sleep until I wake you up. I'll keep the fire going."

The migrants slumped on backpacks or curled up and pulled sweaters and jackets closer for protection against the night chill, but they could not sleep. They were thinking of Don Julio, his grandson and the powerful force that might have compelled them to venture on such a dangerous mission. After a while Borrego said, "Tell us your story, Don Julio." One by one they sat up to listen.

FIVE

Don Julio Escalante

*M*y daughter Lucinda is the reason Manuelito and I are here, but for anyone to understand, I have to first talk about my family. We're from Torreón where I learned the craft of shoemaking and shoe repair from my father, who learned it from his father. In the beginning our family set up a small shoe factory that produced enough to keep my father, mother and their three sons. I was one of them. When I married I stayed with the business and then bought a small home. In time there was enough money to raise a family so that my wife and I had three sons and our daughter Lucinda.

Life was good to us. As the years passed the small factory expanded while my children grew. My sons became men, and no one was surprised when they, too, joined the business and together we set up outlets in the center of town, as well as in the outdoor mercados. In time our business went *beyond the manufacture of shoes into the production of wallets, gloves, belts and handbags. In the meantime, my children married and started their own families. This was good because hard work paid off enough for all of them to have their own homes, children in school, nice clothes for everyone and enough food to share.*

I tell all of this because it's important for you to know that materially everything was fine with our family until anything to do with money started to go wrong. It happened around 1994, when banks lost money overnight, businesses began to wobble, people lost jobs and the economy went bad. Our life, as we used to know it, seemed to collapse. No one could explain what happened except that maybe the gringos and the deals they made with our government had something to do with it.

At first we didn't worry too much about what was happening until people stopped buying our products. Only then did we open our eyes to see how bad things were. There was a lot of gossip and complaining, but most of all, people packed their belongings because they were forced out of family homes. I know all of you have gone through the same thing so I won't talk more about it. I'll just say that our life got hard, very hard.

My family began to feel the hardship when sales started to go down, and we were forced to cut back on clothes, fiestas, piano lessons and, worst of all, food. The only part of the business that remained steady was the shoe repair shop, and that was because people used the same old shoes instead of buying new ones. However, that one shop didn't make enough money to go around. We were a big family.

There was a lot of craziness because no one knew what to do in Torreón. People, trying to save, moved first from street to street, and then out of the city. In the beginning, it wasn't easy for me to know what people were doing. All I saw was that entire families went away. Whenever I asked, I got vague answers, as if something shameful had happened. It was only after time passed that I realized what was happening: families were uprooting and making their way al norte.

My family didn't escape the bad times. We did our best to share what we had, but it was no use. There were too many of us and too few pesos, and, as a last resort, all our children and families moved in with my wife and me. What else could be done? It was better for us to be together under one roof than out on the street alone, and, as you can imagine, the situation soon became nearly impossible. Although the rooms were big enough to be divided for at least a little bit of privacy, the house got too crowded.

Our heart was in it, but living together lasted only a short time. It was too hard. Soon bickering broke out, and the house was filled with the noise of slamming doors and crying people. To make things worse, when the family wasn't arguing over this or that, there was icy silence. I don't know what was worse, the yelling and crying or the terrible stillness. Those were bitter times.

Anyway, that's when my boys and Lucinda's husband decided to migrate to the other side in search of a better life. My boys didn't want to do it, I could tell, but what were they to do? Each one had a family with many responsibilities. They didn't have a choice. When they left, my wife and I thought that it was the worst thing that could happen; that is, until after sometime Lucinda decided that she would follow her husband.

This decision didn't come to her without thinking. I know now that it must have taken her months of considera-

tion and planning. *The idea to join her husband sparked when his first letter came from California, and in it were some American dollars. She became transformed. It was as if her head got filled with dreams of living up there with him, along with their son Manuelito. Those dollars told her that it was possible, that anything was possible. She talked about leaving us, about her new life and about her son learning to speak English.*

That was all Lucinda talked about for months after that letter. I watched her carefully, seeing how she transformed from the ordinary woman who was my daughter into someone almost unknown to me. I saw that her brothers' wives first envied her, and then they laughed at her. They made fun of her. I didn't laugh because I knew in what direction her dreams were dragging her. The more I saw her change, the more I became frightened at the thought of her going out so far by herself.

Lucinda was very special for me. She was our youngest child; she came to us later on, when her brothers were big boys, and from the beginning, I felt a tenderness I had never before known. She was a loving child and a smart one, too. She followed me everywhere just like a little shadow. She soon learned all about shoes and boots and how to repair them. Lucinda was still a little girl but she could already fix a sole, and my customers loved to bring in their shoes just to see the girl at work. As she grew we became very close. We had no secrets. No matter what it was, Lucinda and I always had long conversations about it. This happened when she found the man she wanted to marry, and later on when she was expecting Manuelito. I was the first to know. The truth is that we were friends until she began to plot the trip to join her husband.

The River Flows North

When she revealed her plan I tried to stop her. We talked for hours, for days, and I begged her to wait until things were more stabilized with her husband. I pleaded with her to write to him to see what he had to say about her intentions, but she refused. She knew what he would say, and she didn't want to hear it. In the meantime, I did everything in my power to convince her of the foolishness of what she was going to do. The worst part was that she intended to take Manuelito with her. When I said she should leave the boy behind, she put her hands to her ears to let me know that she would not hear of it. I can't say that she didn't listen to me because I know she did, but her mind was made up; her head was filled with too many dreams of life in the United States.

Everyday I grew more afraid for her because I knew that she was going to risk her life as well as her son's. In the end, however, I found that I didn't have the power to change any part of the nightmare that swallowed us. I think that understanding my powerlessness was the worse part of all.

Not long after, along with Manuelito, she joined the crowds that moved in this direction. When Lucinda and the boy boarded the bus, she promised to write soon, but that didn't happen. We lost contact. There wasn't a word from her, or about her, until one day I received the telephone call. The officer in charge of la Migra on the Mexican side informed me that they had Manuelito in their care, and I had to claim him in Sonoyta.

At first I couldn't make out what this meant. Only Manuelito? Where was his mother? When I asked the man on the phone he said there was no one with the boy. I knew what that meant, but I couldn't accept it. I asked him to look again because I was certain that she was there. Maybe she was standing in the hallway or washing her hands some-

where else. Please look, I asked. I pleaded but my begging went unanswered, and then I knew my girl was dead. When I hung up I put a few things together, left my wife along with the others already grieving for Lucinda and I took the bus to Sonoyta.

Manuelito was nearly a skeleton when I found him. Only his big eyes stared out at me to let me know that he recognized me. He couldn't talk, or maybe it was that he had made up his mind not to talk. Whatever it was, he didn't speak all the way home no matter how much I tried to make him say something. He ate only small pieces of tortillas, and this scared me even more, so I held him in my arms nearly all the way and moved only to walk around the bus whenever it stopped and to help him relieve himself. After a while I didn't ask him anything about what happened to his mother because I thought it might be too painful for him. I decided to wait until later.

When we made it back home, our family and friends had already begun the chain of rosaries for the repose of Lucinda's soul. As you know, that meant that for nine nights we relived Lucinda's death, and we felt that terrible pain over and over. Not only Lucinda's soul was commended to God during those hours of prayer, but the many others who had disappeared without a trace as they tried to cross the desert. Those were nights of sighing and crying that became heavier, more painful each time. Mixed in with the Ave Marías and Padre Nuestros, words were whispered that went straight to my heart.

Voices murmured of the souls that wandered the earth in search of something left behind, spirits whose bodies had never been buried. No one imagined that each word that I overheard was a knife that pierced my heart. Of course, I knew of las ánimas en pena. Who didn't? But I had never given much thought to a soul wandering the earth in misery until now that it was my Lucinda in search of her body.

During the day I visited the cemetery where so many of our family are buried. I did this many times, and each time I was aware of something that filled the air. I didn't know what it was on my first visit. Sighing? Whispers? Weeping? When I returned I knew what it was, and I wasn't frightened because I knew that the voices were my girl's people, clamoring for her bones. I realized then that it wasn't right for her remains to be scattered in an unknown place. That's when the idea began to grow in me, stronger and stronger, until I had to act.

During the period of grieving, Manuelito hardly said a word. He joined in the litanies, in the invocation of saints and martyrs, but he didn't speak of his mother until later when he finally told me of his and Lucinda's ordeal as they crossed the desert. He described how el coyote had abandoned them, and the boy recounted how, after days of walking, his mother fell asleep under a little tree, but she never woke up. When that happened he wandered, lost for a long time, surrounded only by sand as he tried to find help. He couldn't tell if it was hours or days until two gringos dressed in uniforms picked him up and returned him to the Mexican Migra in Sonoyta.

While I listened to Manuelito I didn't say anything because I couldn't. My throat choked with tears. I was so angry that I wanted to reach out across the kilometers into the heart of that devil desert to find my daughter, to help her and bring her back to life. But I couldn't. I was helpless. All I could do was wrestle with my grief and guilt for not having stopped her from leaving. Now I couldn't forgive myself.

Only God could do that much. After a while, something pushed me to get more details from Manuelito, and he said that he remembered where he left his mother. At first I didn't believe what I was hearing, yet because I wanted to believe, I finally did.

Weeks passed, and the thought of Lucinda's body rotting or being devoured by desert beasts grew inside me until it became immense. It became an obsession that robbed me of sleep, and I could hardly eat. The only ordinary thing that filled my days was my shop, where worn-out shoes and boots surrounded me. Bent over my workbench hammering tacks into soles was the only thing that kept me from breaking down, and it was on one of those days that the idea, which had been building inside me, took form. I made up my mind to leave the safety of my home to look for my daughter, and I decided to bring Manuelito with me. I knew that it would be dangerous for him, but I did it because he was the only one who could lead me to his mother.

I'm convinced that he remembers where her bones are, although his memory is not as clear as I thought. We have tried different places, but we have not found her. Not yet, but we will, and we won't give up until we find her. Am I a loco? Well, if I'm crazy maybe God will look down on my craziness and help Manuelito and me.

Anyway, we've been looking for some time now. People have been good to us and helped when we looked in the desert first out of Sonoyta and then out of Los Vidrios. When Manuelito didn't see anything he remembered, we traveled as far as El Saguaro to look and ask, but nothing turned up. Now we've come to La Joyita where we are sure to find her.

SIX

Day Two

Dawn was breaking when Cerda's voice sounded out. "Everybody up! It's time to hit the road."

The group hardly slept after listening to Don Julio's story because his words reminded them of what they, too, had gone through, and this had kept them awake. They got on their feet, went off to relieve themselves and in minutes they were ready.

Cerda stomped out what was left of the small fire, yet he didn't make a move. He lit a cigarette and then scratched his scraggly chin, but still he didn't show signs of moving. After a long pause, he looked at Manuelito and motioned him to come closer. "Tell me what you remember about where your Amá went to sleep."

Everyone looked at one another, not knowing what to think. What was *el coyote* intending? There were a few murmurs, and above it all came Guerrero's voice. "Shit! What are you thinking, Cerda? We better get on the move right now."

"Shut up, Guerrero. Let me think! I'm the *jefe* so don't give me any of your *mierda*. Come here, Manuelito. Tell me what you remember."

The boy moved close to Cerda and repeated what he had told Don Julio. He described boulders and gnarled trees, and when the guide gave him a stick, the boy sketched in the sand what he remembered. Cerda pointed a finger to where they had made camp. "Like these rocks?"

"Sí. But there were two little trees next to them. We got under the shade because the sun was so hot."

"Look over there, *muchacho*. Can you make out the mountains?"

"Sí, Señor."

"Now look at the picture in the sand. Here are the trees. Here are the rocks. Pretend you're looking at them right now, like this." Cerda positioned the boy facing the sketch. "Now tell me. What side of the mountains are you on?"

Manuelito tapped his right shoulder.

Cerda's cagey eyes glowed in the dawn's breaking light. He was hatching a plan, but would not let anyone in on what exactly was on his mind. However, he didn't have to talk because they all had a good idea of what was going on in his mind. "I think I know the place. It's not far from here."

"No! We're paying you to take us to *la Ocho* and not on a tour of this *chingado* desert!" Guerrero's voice was loud and nervous.

The River Flows North

"It's not out of the way, Guerrero. It means making a curve toward the mountains, and then after that goes straight to *la Ocho*. I've done it more than once."

"*Chinga* the curve. You have to take us straight there. You hear me? Straight!" Guerrero's voice was a threat and the rest of the group swiveled around to face him. For a minute he thought that they were hostile, and it convinced him that they were close to jumping him. He backed off.

"Señor Guerrero, calm yourself. Cerda knows what he's doing. Besides him we have another guide, and she will take us to her resting place. Look! There she is again. She's asking us to follow her." Doña Encarnación's voice broke the tension as she pointed in the direction of the mountains, taking everyone's attention away from Guerrero. The group strained to see what the old woman was pointing at, but there was nothing except the first signs of light peeping over the high mountain ridges.

"What are you seeing, Doña Encarnación?" Menda asked what they were all wondering.

"The spirit of the woman that waved at us yesterday. It's Lucinda, and she's telling us to follow her."

"But you said that it was Olga. We crossed her grave." Menda again pressed the point.

"That is what I believed, but I was mistaken. Now I know that it was Lucinda's spirit. Come, Señor Cerda. Let's move. She's impatient."

With all the talk of spirits and graves, Guerrero regained his defiance. "Goddamnit, Cerda! Are you going to make us follow this *vieja loca*? She doesn't know what the hell she's talking about. Shut her up and let's return to the planned route."

"Look, Guerrero," said Menda. "We know what you're talking about, and with all respect, Doña Encarnación and Don Julio, I think the rest of us are entitled to ask some questions about what Cerda's thinking. We're all paying our way, so Cerda should listen to us, too."

"Okay, okay! Don't get all excited! What do you want to know?" Cerda tried to calm down the group.

"Tell us what you're planning," said Menda.

"I'm thinking of going to the place that Manuelito remembers."

"That's crazy, Cerda!" Now the Osuna brothers put in what they were thinking. "Everything looks the same! We'll only get lost!"

An outburst of voices then sounded out fears and complaints, but Cerda responded. "No! It's not crazy. I think I know the place."

"You *think*?" Nicanor shouted.

"All right! I don't just *think!* I know the place. *I know! I know!* You feel better now?"

"You told us that it would take us three days and three nights to reach Ligurta. How will this new plan change that time?" Menda went on questioning.

"It's not going to change anything. Now is the beginning of the second day. Tonight we'll spend the second night at the place Manuelito remembers, and then we head straight for *la Ocho* and Ligurta, getting us there on time. That is, if nothing happens to slow us down."

"If *nothing* happens!" Again the chorus of voices broke into what Cerda was saying. He looked closely at their faces, watching their escalating fears and doubts.

"Relax, everybody! Sometimes things happen. I didn't say they would."

"Like what, Cerda? What things can happen?" Nicanor cried out.

"Aw, shit! Dealing with you is like being with a bunch of stupid kids! What do you think can happen? Somebody breaks a leg, or is bitten by a snake, or falls off a rock, or there's a sandstorm. Crap! Anything can happen! I'm just not saying it will, okay? You got that into your big heads?"

Cerda's quick response silenced the group. They looked at each other hoping to find the answer pasted on somebody's face. Menda finally broke the silence. "Cerda, why are you doing this?"

"Because it's easy."

Not knowing what to make of his response, Menda said, "Give us a few minutes to talk."

The migrants went into a huddle where they whispered. Cerda couldn't hear what they were saying, although he tried to eavesdrop, and he leaned to their side so much at one point that he almost lost his balance. He did see that Guerrero gestured heatedly, but then Menda countered. Doña Encarnación waved toward the mountains, and everyone listened. Then the Osuna brothers jabbered something, and they all nodded in agreement. Celia held her fisted hands on her hips and said something that took more time than the others, apparently turning the tide. They finally came to an agreement and returned to Cerda.

"Okay, Cerda, we agree, but only for Don Julio and Manuelito." Menda looked at the old man and the boy, letting them know that they were the reason they had agreed to take what they considered a dangerous detour.

"Goddammit! Have you all gone crazy?" Guerrero's voice was a mix of rage and panic. "What are the odds of this *pendejo coyote* finding another place that looks just like this one? The one where that stupid woman croaked? Think, *idiotas*. What are the odds? Zero! That's what!"

Cerda ignored Guerrero's outburst and, followed closely by Don Julio and Manuelito, started to walk in an easterly direction. The rest of the group did the same. Guerrero, still resentful, dragged his feet and mumbled obscenities as he tagged along because he had no other choice. No one spoke. They were filled with a renewed energy that kept them from remembering that they were tired, thirsty and nervous about the unplanned change.

That was in the beginning because, as hours passed, their strength dripped away, and their feet grew heavier. They struggled with the deep sand that sometimes nearly swallowed a leg up to the knee. The sun beat down on them with relentless heat, drenching bodies in sweat, parching and cracking lips. The wind blasted dust devils into their faces and forced them to halt to rub sand from their squinting, burning eyes. Thirst intensified and caused their tongues to swell. Although they tried to hold back, they had no choice but to take sips from jugs that became emptier. Still, they managed to keep on their feet although they fell behind Cerda whose pace grew faster with each hour. Only Don Julio and Manuelito trailed close to him.

As the sun dipped to the west, the group finally began to make out the distant outline of boulders. After a while stunted, gnarled ironwood trees came into view. When they got to the site, they flopped on the sand: some on their knees, others flat on their bellies with heads burrowed into crossed arms, some panting and coughing. The only ones who remained on their feet were Cerda and Don Julio who held up Manuelito. When the old man gave his grandson a questioning look, the boy nodded. This signal revived everyone, and they stared at the sight; eyes looked from boulders to trees, and back to the boulders as if expecting to find Lucinda waiting for them. Instead they saw nothing except shifting sand. No one uttered a sound. Only the wind hissed through tiny crevices etched into the boulders' surface.

"Her bones are here." Doña Encarnación spoke in a steady voice as she looked around, sweeping the area with an outstretched arm. The others looked, but couldn't make out anything until Celia, drawn to an object sticking out of the sand, went to it, got on her knees, dug around it and then yanked. The remnants of a faded sneaker dangled from her fingers.

"Abuelo, that's hers. It's Amá's shoe." Manuelito's voice was shrill with excitement as he ran to Celia who handed him the shoe. "She's here! She's here!" Like a puppy digging in search of a buried bone, Manuelito got on his knees and clawed with all his strength, spraying sand into the air. The rest followed, and they dug haphazardly, without knowing what would come up. Borrego found a branch that he handled like a shovel, but the rest used only their hands. Guerrero gawked at the frenzy with a look of disbelief mingled with scorn. He didn't help. Instead he lit a cigarette and slumped under one of the scrawny trees, smirking at the group's stupidity.

Cerda was the first to come up with a bone. The migrants stopped, panting and sweating from the exertion. Most shrank back, frightened by what *el coyote* held in his hand. "Don Julio, I think this was an arm, but if I was you I wouldn't bet that it belongs to Lucinda. This desert is loaded with bones. All someone has to do is scratch a little to find something that used to be a man or a woman. I brought you here because I think this is where your daughter ended her trip, but that doesn't mean this is her bone."

Don Julio moved closer to Cerda, reverently taking the bone from his hands. It was obvious that he wasn't listening to *el coyote*'s words of caution and that he instead chose to believe that it was part of his daughter's body. The old man went to his backpack, took out a folded burlap sack and carefully put the bone inside it. In seconds, everyone went back to digging, this time with renewed strength.

One by one things turned up. The ragged remains of a woman's trousers, faded pink in color. Another bone, this time what must have been a leg. Then a sweater sleeve was found. Each time a piece of clothing was discovered, Manuelito shouted out, "It's hers!" As the hours passed, more things came up; small pieces of personal articles, but most important, several large bones were collected. As these were handed to him, Don Julio quietly put each one into the sack.

"Okay! Everybody stop." Cerda shouted out in a tone of voice that said that he had nearly forgotten his role of guide. "We're going to die of fatigue and thirst if we don't take a break. Stop until I say we can start again. Just lay down, drink some water and rest. I don't think there's much more left, so we'll look a while longer and then give up. It's soon going to get dark anyway. We can camp here."

Cerda had barely finished speaking when Menda held out something. It was a skull. There was a gasp as Don Julio leaped to take it from her, holding it with the reverence of a priest holding a chalice. The old man looked at his companions, and he held the skull pointed at them, as if introducing her. "This is Lucinda, my daughter."

The River Flows North

"No, Don Julio, you can't be sure. It could be anybody." Cerda again voiced doubt, but it was clear that the old man wasn't listening. Instead he went to sit under a tree while he cradled the skull as he had held Lucinda when she was an infant. Everyone stood by watching him rock his arms as he moved his lips, but it was impossible to hear what he was saying. After a while he got to his feet and went to each one and embraced and thanked them for their help. They all responded with small remarks demonstrating that they were glad to have been part of finding Lucinda's remains.

"Hey! Cerda! Let's get the hell out of here. We've wasted enough time on this crap."

"Shut up, Guerrero!" Cerda snapped back. "I'm tired of your whining. Why don't you help us instead of standing there like a *pendejo.*"

"Yeah, Guerrero! Shut up!" The others, fed up with the complainer, followed Cerda's lead in shouting down Guerrero. The man again shrank back and stayed that way as Cerda told everyone to break for camp. They silently collected kindling for a fire and soon gathered around it.

Exhausted yet stimulated by the discovery and convinced that the remains were Lucinda's, they sat silently around the fire. This night there would be no singing or dancing; only the crackling of burning branches mingled with the sound of gusting wind filled their silence. The only movements were hands that reached for a bit of jerky wrapped in a tortilla and then swallowed down with sips of water. Eyes were riveted on the dancing flames of the campfire, but their thoughts were wrapped around bones they had discovered, on Don Julio's loving hands and on Manuelito's yelps of joy each time anything was unearthed. Now and then glances were exchanged, followed by a faint smile. Most of them looked at

Don Julio and Manuelito to let them know that they were encouraged by the find because it gave each of them renewed hope.

As the moon slid closer to its highest point, one by one the migrants reclined on backpacks or on crossed arms. Fatigue finally overcame them, and they began to slip into sleep when Don Julio startled them. They sat up to see that he was on his feet rousing Manuelito.

"What are you doing, Don Julio?" Cerda's voice sounded more anxious than curious.

"The boy and I are leaving."

"What do you mean?" Without answering, the old man gathered his things and at the same time made sure that Manuelito was on his feet. He picked up the burlap sack with Lucinda's remains and flung it over his shoulder.

"We're very grateful to all of you, but as I said before, Manuelito and I have what we came for, so now we're going back home."

"I can't let you do that, Don Julio." Cerda was now standing at arm's reach of the old man.

"This is what we came for, and now we're going back home."

Cerda said something, but it was drowned out by all the other voices begging Don Julio not to leave. They were now on their feet, and they moved closer to him, some hands even clasped the old man's arms. A babble of voices hit him from every side.

"You and the boy will die out there."

"You'll lose your way and die of thirst and exhaustion."

"There are snakes that might get at you, even vultures."

"Don Julio, think of the boy."

"At least wait until daylight."

The River Flows North

The pounding voices grew in intensity and loudness until the old man raised his hands. "Amigos, thank you, but we have to leave right now because every minute is precious. My wife is waiting for us to return. We won't get lost. I made sure to watch out for signs that will lead us back to La Joyita. Please don't be afraid for us."

Don Julio's voice was steady and assured, silencing everyone. Even Cerda stepped back to look at the old man with admiration. He scratched his head and finally nodded. "You're as stubborn as a mule and I can't stop you. Okay! Just make sure to keep the mountains on your left. When the sun comes up it should be on your left, too. Stick to that and you'll make it. Remember, you're not going back on the same path we took getting here. We curved, but if you keep the mountains and sun like I told you, you'll make it. And you, *muchacho*, watch where you step. Okay?"

"Sí, Señor Cerda." Manuelito's voice was soft, but clear.

The old man went to each one of the migrants, embraced and shook hands. When he approached Doña Encarnación, she took his hands and held them. "You have a guide, don't forget. She's your daughter, and she won't let you or her son die."

"Doña Encarnación, I don't have your eyes to see her. I want to, but I can't."

"Yes, you can. Believe and you'll see her. Follow her and I promise that she will lead you to La Joyita. I know that you will reach your wife."

"Gracias, Doña Encarnación."

Don Julio, with backpack in place, Manuelito held by the hand and the burlap sack slung over his shoulder, walked away. The migrants watched as he and the boy slipped into the darkness; soon the two silhouettes vanished into the sighing wind.

That night as Don Julio and Manuelito disappeared into the gloom, Armando Guerrero took a hard look at what he was certain were a couple of losers. What he saw were a dumpy old man and a useless boy who had risked their lives, and for what? A bag of bones! Armando laughed as the old goat shuffled into the darkness, just as he scoffed at the other dreamers sprawled out around him because he thought that they were a pack of fools. After a while he pushed his thoughts aside and he checked his own bag, making sure it was zipped tight and secure. Guerrero stretched out on his back and used the bag like a pillow. He settled in for a good sleep, but after a long time he saw that it was useless. There was too much going on in his head even for a short doze.

SEVEN

Armando Guerrero

*T*onalá is in Jalisco. I was born there. The town is so close to Guadalajara that most people think that it's a barrio of that city, but that's not so because Tonalá is Tonalá. It has its own mayor, its school and way too many poor people. The only things that give the town something to brag about are its pottery factories and rows of restaurants buzzing with roaming mariachi bands; all the crap that tourists love.

My father's name was Gonzalo Guerrero and my mother's name was Felicia. He was a waiter in one of those tourist restaurants, and she took in laundry while she had a kid every year. Both of them worked like burros just to feed the litter they brought into this world, but they never complained. Burros never complain.

I am the last of nine brothers and sisters. We were so many that hardly anyone could remember our names, not *even our mother. We were a bunch of poor raggedy brats, the poorest family in Tonalá. When I was old enough to see that I was born into pure chicken-shit poverty, I was ashamed of my family, and I wanted to get out of it.*

As the years passed, I felt more pissed and hardly ever satisfied with what came my way. I remember that there was always something eating at my guts, something down deep inside me. I hated everything, especially the beat-up school I went to along with all the other barrio kids, the older ones, little ones, stupid ones and cross-eyed ones. Age didn't matter. We were all thrown into one room with a teacher who was always half crocked on tequila.

My older brothers were expected to bring in money to help out. They shined shoes, washed car windows or picked up trash, but they didn't make much of a difference at home because they were a bunch of idiots. Most of the time they just bummed around and returned to my mother with empty pockets. I used to watch them all the time and thought they were stupid for wasting their time.

When I was about seven years old I decided to show them how to do things. At first, I followed them when they ditched school. It was easy; we just sneaked out the door while the old fart snored at his desk. I saw that once we were out on the streets, the guys started to treat me like I was grown up, and that's when things turned around.

Although I was just a little shit, already I had better ideas than the older guys. I'm the one who thought of hitting the pottery dumps to dig for rejects and then washing those ashtrays and candleholders until they looked almost new. On top of that, it was my idea to take the junk to where gringo tourists hung out, where we were sure to sell our things.

The River Flows North

I always came up with ideas. I remember the time I bet the guys that if I smiled real cute some gringa old bag would buy whatever I had in my hand. When they said that I couldn't pull it off, I did, and it worked. After that they paid attention to whatever I said or did. They watched my moves and tried to do what I did. I found out that I could charm anyone right out of their socks if I tried. One cute smile kept the centavos rolling in my direction.

My brothers started right away in the business that I planned, and in no time we usually put together twenty-five centavos here and a peso over there. At the end of each day we went home with a good stash. They hated it, but my brothers had to admit that even though I was the smallest of the family, I was the smartest.

We pulled off our little jobs for a while, but then I got to thinking that it wasn't fair that I wasn't getting something extra for my ideas. It hit me that if I charged just a couple of more centavos for each pottery piece I could keep it for myself, and nobody would know the difference. After a while, the coins built up, and I felt real good just walking down those shitty streets listening to the coins jingle in my pocket.

I worked that way until I was around twelve when everything got boring: my brothers, the crappy rejects, the chicken-shit coins and especially school, where I wasted hours just looking at the old drunk. So I dumped the whole thing, including school and work with my brothers. I didn't tell anybody at home about my change, and even though they saw what I was doing, they never got a peep out of me. Why should I explain anything? It wasn't anybody's business.

I got myself a job washing dishes and cleaning tables at a restaurant. In the beginning I thought I made a mistake because it was hard work, but once I caught on I started to watch the people that filled the place. I checked out the gringos who were always laughing and throwing dollars all over the place. Besides them, the ones that really caught my eye were the mexicanos, the business guys that flashed even bigger rolls than the gringos, and I caught on that beautiful girls always hung around them.

That bunch really got to me, and I tried to work the tables closest to them. If one guy needed a light, I was there with a match. If another wanted one more shot, I had the bottle right there. I hung around the mexicanos so much that I started to walk like them, even talk like them. I kept my ears open all the time, and I discovered that those guys were narcos and traficantes, as the other waiters called them, but I wasn't afraid of them. In fact, I wanted to be part of them.

Those guys dressed real sharp. Anybody could tell that their suits were American. They wore slick shirts with fancy ties and expensive shoes. Whenever a hand reached into a pocket for a wallet crammed with dollars, the fingers were loaded with diamond rings. They drove flashy American cars, too. What else could anybody expect? But what really nailed me was when I saw for the first time that those narcos packed guns. I saw this by accident when I happened to be standing next to one of them as he reached into his pocket. That's when I caught only a glimpse, but I knew what it was.

I was only twelve or thirteen, but already I noticed the women that hung around those men. They were beautiful, with ruby-colored lips, and they were always smiling, showing off big white teeth. They wore their hair long, and they dressed in tight outfits that showed off their butts and boobs. What I could hardly believe were the high-heeled slinky shoes they wore because I could tell that it was hard for them

The River Flows North

to keep their balance. The more I looked at those women, and the guys that paid their way, the more I wanted to be part of the whole thing.

I grew up fast, and I got what I wanted. By the time I was eighteen or nineteen, I was on the pay. At first, I was a gofer and drove jefes around town and made drops of coca, but most of all I delivered fat bundles of money. I knew that being a delivery boy was the bottom step of that work and just chicken shit, but I wanted to be part of the outfit. I told myself that in a couple of years I'd be up there with the toughest of the dogs. In the meantime, I did everything I could to look and think like those traficantes because I wanted so bad to be one of them.

It wasn't long before I got to be one of the favorites. In fact, I became the best runner. I made real good money, too, and now it was me who wore the silk suits and shirts and even a diamond ring on my little finger. I must have looked pretty sharp because women always gave me the big eye whenever I got close to the jefes. I pretended not to notice because I knew it was risky business messing with those women, but I did it anyway because I couldn't help myself. On my time off, I always had a woman with me when I went to private clubs to dance and drink whiskey.

I didn't live at home anymore. I got myself a classy-looking apartment down the street from the cathedral where all the action went on in downtown Guadalajara. The truth was that I just couldn't be at home anymore. I hated the shabby little rooms and the stink that came out of the kitchen and toilet. Besides, my brothers weren't as stupid as I thought. They caught on to what I was doing, and they made my mother nag me because I didn't work, but still I had money and clothes. Where did the money come from?

Where? Where? She was on top of me all the time, and I couldn't stand it. Things got even worse when my brothers' jobs dried up, and all they did was sit around the kitchen table bellyaching about how bad things were going for them.

I didn't think it could get worse until they started to bullshit about making it up to the other side to find work. The worst part was that they weren't happy enough to talk just for themselves. No, Señor. It wasn't long before they started in on me and tried to get me to join them on the road to el norte. When I saw that they were serious I told them they were crazy, that I wasn't cut out to work like a mule digging ditches or washing cars for the gringos. I walked away from them whenever they started to nag me, happy that I didn't have to do that kind of shit.

I finally walked away from the family when I was about twenty-two. I was still young, but by then I had a real handle on the business, and I was more than just a delivery boy by then. Now I was quick on the selling of the coca and dealing with the money. Everyday I got in deeper and hustled for myself and for the big dogs. I liked it although I always thought that something bigger, something better was going to happen to me, so I waited. I don't know for what. I just waited.

Then years slipped by, but I kept doing the same thing. I pushed stuff, handled money, made drops and drove the big shitheads around. That's when I started getting bored, just like when I was a kid, digging up shitty pottery rejects to sell to some skinny gringas for a handful of centavos. It wasn't too long before I started getting impatient especially when I had to face the fact that no matter how many silk suits I got, no matter how many babes I slept with, I was still just a messenger boy getting nowhere.

The River Flows North

I wanted more everyday, and that's when ideas again started to move around in my head. The more I thought of it, the more I saw that I was smarter than all of those chingones put together, but I was still nothing more than a punk peddler. I saw that the real money floated all around me, just like oxygen, except it never made it into my hands; all I got was chicken feed. The worst part of all was when it hit me that nobody really saw how smart I was.

It was a dicey time for me so I tried to scare those thoughts away. At first I hated thinking like that because those ideas made me real nervous. I knew that I was messing with fire, but then the day came when I shoved all that nervous bullshit away. I got rid of anything that made me jittery, and I started to hatch a plan. I figured out exactly when I'd run off with just one of those big money deliveries. It would be easy. All I had to do was what I did every day, the difference would be that instead of driving the load to the place where I was supposed to, I would head straight to the border.

Okay, I knew that stealing was the worst thing for that pack of jackals, but what did anybody expect? Did they think I'd stick around to drive cars and sell little chicken-shit stashes for the rest of my life? Or was I expected to follow my brothers' tracks, get married to some girl who would hatch a brat every nine months, always waiting for me to bring in stinking beans and tortillas year in and year out? Worse, did anybody think that I was about to swim across some lousy river just to get into the United States to work like a goddamn burro?

It took me just a few months to jump into the plan. I got rid of all those bullshit ideas that were making me afraid. I decided to head for the border, and I would do it with class, just like I was a tourist. I decided not to take anything except a big bag filled with bills and a loaded pistol. One million American dollars was the usual load, and that's how much would be in my bag. My plan was to drive my load to Tijuana where planes took off all the time for Los Angeles. From there I would head for Canada. After that who knew what was next?

The fastest route out of Jalisco toward California heads north and hugs the coast through Mazatlán, so that's the road I took. Shit! I was the happiest guy in the world until things started to go wrong almost right away. When I pulled into a gas station on the outskirts of Guaymas, I caught sight of the stinking pair of goons. It wasn't a mistake because right away I recognized the stiff walk, the shades and the bulges sticking out from under the jackets.

¡Mierda! When I saw them, I got confused and spooked because I could have sworn that my plan was airtight. I jumped into the car and pulled away from the gas station like a thousand devils were on my tail, all the time asking myself over and over what went wrong. Where did I mess up? I couldn't figure it out. All I knew was that I had to get the hell out of there fast. I backtracked to get on the connecting road that goes east to Delicias, and from there north to Chihuahua. All the time I was thinking that I would be nothing but dog meat if I didn't shake off those son of a bitches. I was so goddamn scared that I could barely keep my eyes off the rearview mirror, and my hands shook so bad that I could hardly drive the goddamn car.

I was scared shitless, so I ran for it and drove like a loco until I reached Chihuahua where it looked like I had gotten rid of the goons. I dumped the car and lugged my bag to the bus station where I got on the first bus out of there. I didn't care where the thing was going, and it wasn't until the bus was already on the road that I found out it was headed for Sonoyta. It turned out to be the end of the line, and because I needed to keep on the move I hitchhiked back to La Joyita, the truck stop I heard people say was the start of the shortest route across the desert. I hadn't figured on making that crossing, but what the hell? I didn't have a choice.

When I got to La Joyita, I was still shaky so I hung around and burned time to make sure that I wasn't followed. I kept looking everywhere but there was nothing so I finally edged up to a bunch of losers that listened to a skinny guy who called himself Leonardo Cerda. I stood by for a while until I decided that this was the coyote for me.

EIGHT

Day Three

"We're abandoned! Cerda ran off! We're dead!" Nicanor jolted his *compañeros* with a scream. They scrambled to their knees until they managed to get on their feet, all of them half asleep, trying to make sense of why the Osuna brother was crying out.

"Settle down, Nicanor. You've had a bad dream!" Menda tried to keep calm, but her eyes darted from one side of the campsite to the other. She shuffled to where she had last seen Cerda before she fell asleep. When she finished searching in the dim light of dawn, she saw that he was gone. As soon as that sunk in, her head snapped in the direction of where Guerrero had sprawled out overnight. He, too, was gone. A torrent of groans and obscenities was unleashed when the migrants understood the situation. They knew right away; it was not unusual. The double-crossing *coyote* had betrayed them.

Daylight was barely creeping over the mountains, and they wailed when the gravity of what was happening hit them. They had been warned, they knew about the treachery of *coyotes,* but they had not allowed themselves to imagine that it could happen to them. With the exception of Doña Encarnación, their voices grew more and more shrill as terror gripped them, and they forgot about one another. They thought only of themselves and how they would perish in that desolate wilderness. They thought about the grief it would cause their families. Suddenly they became quiet, silenced by a strong whistle of the wind that came from nowhere only to disappear just as mysteriously.

After a while, Menda spoke. Her voice was troubled yet steady, "Listen, *compañeros,* we have to take control of ourselves if we want to live. Sit down and let's talk." Her words had a force that sucked in their attention, and they stared at her. They did not know what to think except that there was something in her face and voice that calmed them so they stopped moaning. One by one, her companions flopped on their haunches ready to listen. "First of all, we have to keep calm so we can think straight."

"Keep calm? Think straight? Are you crazy, Menda? Don't you see that we're in the middle of the desert and we don't know what direction to go?" Nicanor, without thinking, spoke up.

"That's right! How in the hell are we going to reach *la Ocho* without that piece of shit?" said Celia.

Borrego joined in until all three were again shouting and screaming, their voices high-pitched and filled with anxiety. They pelted Menda with words as if she had been the guilty one. They jabbered at once without listening to what they were saying. Doña Encarnación, who had been quiet from the beginning, glared at Celia and then at Nicanor and Borrego. She stared them down until they became still. "Listen to Menda."

However, the panic had by now rubbed off on Menda, and she found herself nearly unable to speak. She made a sign with her hand telling them to wait until she steadied. They stared at her, and then at each other, hoping that someone would think of a way out. When no one spoke, they withdrew into themselves to discover that they, too, had been struck speechless from fear. Their tongues had become numb and stiff. In the meantime, their silence was filled with gusts of wind that blew from the west. Each blast grew stronger and hotter, but still they sat stunned into gloomy stillness. Finally Menda found her voice. "Cerda is gone, but that doesn't mean that we're going to die. We can make a plan."

"Like what?" Nicanor snapped.

"Look, what was the last thing Cerda told Don Julio?" As she spoke Menda raised her arm toward the still black mountains. "Keep those mountains always on your left side. They're your guide. Remember that? Well, since we're going in the opposite direction, what we have to do is keep them on our right side. This is our third day when Cerda said we would reach *la Ocho* and from there Ligurta. This means that we're close. We can make it, I tell you, but we must stay calm."

They looked at one another. They were thinking hard, their brows furrowed as her words took shape and after a while they realized that what she said made sense. One by one, their bodies expressed relief.

The River Flows North

"Menda's right. We have water for one more day and enough to eat." Borrego's optimism returned, connecting with the rest of the group. "We can make it!" He looked to the mountains where the sun's blistering rays were growing brighter. "I say that we get going and that we'd better do it before it really starts to burn. We've already lost valuable time, and who knows, maybe we can even catch up with those two *ratas*. What do you say?"

Borrego's hopefulness worked. Fear lessened, giving way to something close to calm; no one said it, but they knew that they had no alternative. They had to try to get out of the desert so that they could live, and Menda's plan was the best they had. Without saying anymore, the band got to their feet, strapped on their belongings and began the trek with Menda in the lead. It promised to be a clear day, easy to keep the mountains as their compass. With lowered heads they silently marched, energized by the hope that maybe they would sleep in Ligurta that night, once again surrounded by other human beings instead of the desert's intolerable desolation.

Hours later they came to a cluster of saguaro cactus, and their long branches cast arm-like shadows on the sand where the weary travelers found protection. The wind had become stronger so they agreed it was a good place to take shelter and rest. Everyone made sure that the mountains were still where they should be.

Sounds of clicking water jug tops followed by soft sipping and gurgling filled the air. A piece of jerky and tortilla along with talk of what it was going to be like to walk into Ligurta renewed their energy. After a while, Celia noticed that the wind had picked up, and she wondered what they should do about it, but the others did not pay attention to it. Instead they heaved insults on *el pinche coyote* and cursed the day he was born. They had special words for Guerrero, too.

"Why did Cerda abandon us? He could have collected all his money in just a few hours. What got into him?" Of them all, Nicanor was the most intrigued by the question, and he talked, as if to himself. "I think it was that piece of shit Guerrero. He must have bribed him with more money than what we would have paid him."

"What if Cerda didn't want to go?" Doña Encarnación broke in. "What if it wasn't money that made him go?"

"What do you mean, Doña Encarnación?" Menda pressed the old woman.

"Maybe Cerda was kidnapped."

The idea of a *coyote* being snatched from his group was so unheard of and strange that everyone except the old lady snorted and groaned with disbelief.

"What I mean is that he did not show signs of intending to betray us. One can feel treachery."

"Feel? How can anyone *feel* treachery?" Nicanor's voice was edged with sarcasm.

"I can, and I did not feel it in Cerda."

They gawked at the old lady and wagged their heads. They could not agree with her because they saw only the obvious: *El coyote* had dumped them and run off with that other scumbag Guerrero. Respect, however, held them back from contradicting her, so they kept quiet and prepared to take a short nap.

Then, in an instant it happened. An ear-splitting boom cracked somewhere in the west. In seconds a deafening bang followed, sounding so close that it seemed to explode above them, gashing at the air like countless thunders. Along with the relentless booming, a shrill whistle cut through the air, and this time it was on top of them. Their eyes snapped toward the west where they saw a giant wave of sand rolling in their direction at incredible speed.

Horrified and hardly believing their eyes, they sought shelter from that deluge of roiling sand coming at them, but there was nowhere to find cover except by crouching as close as possible to the trunks of the saguaros and bunching on top of one another. No one knew how it happened. Arms lashed out desperately to grab an anchor, anything that provided gravity against the wind that whipped at them. Arms linked with arms, legs intertwined with legs and they held each other fast, driven by instinct to resist being dragged away.

The wind slammed into them as if it had been a solid wall, scratching and tearing any part of their body that was not protected by a sweater or shirt. They huddled against the wind, lips pressed tight, eyes snapped shut and faces turned away, feebly trying to protect heads from being battered by the lacerating sand. It swirled so thick and heavy that it eclipsed the sun and blocked all light until the day became dark as night. All the time the ear-splitting booms of the enraged wind thrashed them while it whipped and churned the desert floor.

No one could tell how long the storm lasted, whether it was minutes or an eternity. All they knew was when it was finally over. The howling, cracking wind passed as fast as it had come, and it raced away leaving behind only its terrifying echo. Horrified, they watched as the hurtling wind dragged away the deadly wave of sand that had punished everything in its path, and from there they could see it spiraling hundreds of feet upward, creating a ceiling so thick that not even a glimpse of sky was visible. As the wind passed, a gloomy stillness was left behind. Weak rays of daylight slowly sifted through the dense roof of sand only to disappear into darkness.

Still clinging to one another, they began to move. Like a child who had let himself be buried playing on the beach, Nicanor showed his head above the sand. Soon the others found that they, too, were sunk up to their shoulders. Eyes blinked open, and heads shook off wads of sand. Bodies wiggled and swiveled. Arms tugged and pushed until one by one limbs came free, and everyone dug out from under the heavy load of sand. They grunted, sneezed and coughed to clear their throats of the sand that had filtered all the way under their tongues.

When finally they were above ground, they looked at each other's faces and saw bloated masks whitened by the blast. Their eyes were sunk into dark sockets, and their hair was spiked around spots that were scraped bald. Blotches of blood showed where the sand had scraped off skin, most of their fingers were bleeding and their clothes were rags barely covering their bodies. They huddled against one another as they cried and moaned, hardly believing they were still alive. After a while, Menda pointed, "Look, over there."

"What?" Celia's voice was a croak.

"The saguaros." Borrego caught on and answered Celia's question. "They're far away."

Almost at once, they realized that they had been dragged several yards from the saguaros, but that it had happened to all of them at the same time because they clung to each other with such ferocity.

"Wait a minute! Where's Doña Encarnación?" Celia missed the old woman.

"¡Dios Santo! What happened to her?" Menda jumped from where she crouched and turned in a circle; her eyes darted from one side to the other. The others yelled out the woman's name but there was nothing, only the stillness that remains after a storm. They shouted and waited, hoping to hear the old lady call out, but after a while they understood that Doña Encarnación was gone, buried somewhere under tons of sand. Still, their eyes went on scanning the desolation. They tried to detect at least a slight ripple, a movement to give them a clue, but only the flat whiteness of newly sifted sand glared back at them. One after the other began to mutter, but their voices were so soft they were almost whispering. First it was Nicanor, then Borrego, then Celia.

"Let's go out and look for her."

"Where do we start?"

"I don't know, but we should try to find her."

The chatter stopped when they realized that a search would be futile, above all dangerous. Then Borrego noticed something. "Look! The mountains are gone!"

Everyone reacted without noticing that they were each staring in a different direction. When they did realize it, a horrible reality hit them: The mountains weren't gone, rather it was that the sandstorm that nearly killed them had veiled the mountains, obscuring them from view and now there was nothing to guide them. Their main compass had vanished, making everything look the same no matter which direction they faced. Each one turned in a slow circle facing all sides, trying to detect anything that would give them a bearing, but there was nothing. The sun was obscured, as were the mountains, and they realized that they were utterly disoriented. Understanding this filled them with a terror none had ever experienced, because they understood that now they were truly and hopelessly lost.

Struggling to fight off panic, Menda spoke up. Her voice was hoarse with tension. "Look, the saguaros were on our left when the storm hit. That means that they were on our west side and they haven't moved so that gives us direction."

"How can we be sure? We were dragged a long way from the cactus." Nicanor's eyes were filled with terror as he stammered. "How do we know in what direction. How can we know where are we standing right now? Maybe we're north or maybe even south of the saguaros."

"We were dragged in the direction the wind was blasting and that was to the east," Celia mumbled.

"I felt like the wind was going in circles," Borrego broke in.

"No! No! It was going in a straight path. That way, toward *la Ocho*," Menda insisted.

The jabbering escalated, voices contradicting one another. No one was listening, and they became more hysterical with each moment. Fear intensified when, suddenly stunned into silence, they realized that their belongings had been swept away. Nothing had been left behind, and their backpacks, where they had stashed rations of food, were gone. When they fumbled for the belt or the pack safeguarding their funds, they discovered that it, too, had been ripped away by the wind. Most important, every water jug had disappeared.

"We're dead!" Nicanor had reached the end and felt that he could no longer hope to make it out alive. Celia collapsed on the sand, listless and with nothing to say because she, too, had lost faith. Borrego looked from his brother to Celia to Menda, not ready to give in to despair. He seemed to expect that someone would say that things would be all right and that there was a way out. Menda looked at him, and she seemed to read his thoughts.

The River Flows North

"I know what we can do. Let's wait here until the sand clears so that we can see the mountains again. It can't take that long, maybe just a few hours. In the meantime, if we stay here we can get back some strength and then start walking again. We're close."

Nicanor, still in the grip of deep fear, lashed out at Menda. "Look, I don't know who you are, but I'm not ready to go on doing things your way. You've told us what to do for a long time, and I'm not going to listen anymore. Why should I follow you?"

Menda went to Nicanor and put her face so close to his that he felt her breath on his cheeks. She glared into his eyes, hardly blinking. When she spoke, her voice was stern. "You're going to follow me because I'm old enough to be your mother, and just like you would follow her, you're going to follow me. What would you have us do? Go out there and run around in circles until we drop dead from thirst and hunger? Is that what you want?"

"No, Señora."

"Do you have a better plan?"

"No," Nicanor responded quietly, even respectfully, but his body showed that he resented being put in that position.

"Okay, let's go to the saguaros. Maybe we can find some liquid inside them." Menda showed that she knew what he was feeling. "Does anybody have a knife to cut into the trunks?"

Celia and the brothers followed Menda as she led them to the cactus, but Celia and Nicanor dragged behind, their spirits draining out of them with each step. Nicanor handed his pocketknife to Menda, and she dug as deep as she could until she found small pockets of a gummy fluid that they took turns licking. Then one by one they flopped onto the sand, either asleep or unconscious.

When they awoke, it was nighttime, and the sky was so black that they knew the sand had not yet cleared. Menda and Borrego were able to rip off dry growth from the cactus, and when she found a pack of matches in her pocket she set a small fire. Then they huddled around it, feeling that its radiance revived them, its puny flames filled them with some energy. Menda waited to speak until all were fully awake. "I'm thinking of Doña Encarnación. I feel that she's somewhere close to us even if we can't see her."

"I don't feel sorry for her." Nicanor was the only one to speak up. "She did what she wanted."

"What are you talking about?" Celia whispered, sounding a bit shocked.

"*Bueno*. She said that she was coming to the desert to stay with the spirits. Remember? She said it from the beginning. I think Doña Encarnación is with them now."

Faint crackling came from the fire, and the four listened to it as if it was Doña Encarnación's voice. They were trying to get some hope from what might have been the old woman's words had she still been with them. Menda, sensing their depression, wanted to fight it off although she, too, was afraid. "We have to have her faith. Maybe we'll be able to see her spirit or others who will lead us out of this desert."

No one responded, instead they gathered closer to the fire, each one listening to the desert's night sounds and the soft whistling of the dreaded wind. The four had been left alive by the sandstorm, but they knew that they were lost. They were thirsty, bruised and cut, and so stiffened from the pounding the storm had inflicted on them that they were certain that without *el coyote* they would not get out alive and that not even the presence of a guiding spirit could save them.

Menda understood. She slid down on her side, careful not to press the parts of her body that ached the most. She closed her eyes, staying that way for the rest of the night. She was tired and desperately in need of sleep, but her mind was too alert, so she spent the long night listening to the sighs that drifted in the darkness. She knew Doña Encarnación was out there and that she was looking over them. Menda knew also that the old woman was not alone. Alongside her were the ones she had come to meet.

NINE

Doña Encarnación Padilla

I *belong to the Lacandona people that inhabit that vast jungle located on the southernmost tip of Mexico. I was named Encarnación because from the beginning the wise ones of my tribe designated me to be the one in whom our ancestors, los tatuches, would take flesh. What my people saw in time was that there was something that made me unique: I was a dreamer. This was a special sign because the Lacandona people hold the belief that in dreams the ancestors communicate wisdom and guidance, and when someone is blessed as a dreamer, that person is considered a gifted messenger, the voice of the ancestors. As soon as I was able to express my dreams, although still a child, it was expected by the elders that I sit with them, and tell what los tatuches had communicated.*

Through the years I told of dreams that revealed future days of yet more turmoil and suffering, of displacement and

The River Flows North

uprisings against los patrones, the plantation owners, who relentlessly drove the Lacandona people. I spoke of coming warfare throughout Chiapas, a struggle greater than the one fought against the first bearded conquistadores. The elders listened to my words, knowing that it was what our ancestors were saying, and they always wanted to know more.

When questioned even more, I told of dreams that showed future migrations to the land of our beginnings, a return to the northern deserts from where our ancestors had come. I also told of the dream that showed me joining such a migration, and it was about this journey that the wise ones became most interested because they wanted to know about the future of our people.

There were other matters on which the elders often consulted me; they wanted to hear of the past as well. In response I shared more images that I dreamed, such as past migrations south from distant lands, and our people's entry into the jungle. For the elders, this was important since they knew that people and events repeat themselves in endless cycles. When I spoke they linked my dreams together, the ones about the past alongside the ones about the future.

My dreams, however, did not keep me from living an ordinary life. I was the younger of two daughters, but my appearance encouraged the man who would be my husband to skip my older sister in his petition to marry me. I was fourteen years old, an age thought to be right, so in exchange for two goats, I was married and I soon had my first child, a son. I went on to live a life of having children, fishing in the rivers and planting, and weaving small articles to sell in San Cristóbal de las Casas. My life was always the same until the day that my destiny shifted its direction, leading me to ven-

*ture into what was forbidden for any Lacandona woman. At
that time, I was no longer a girl, but neither was I old.*

*It happened on a hot day when I neared the river hoping
to find some coolness. I waded into the water up to my hips,
wetting my head and shoulders until my blouse clung to my
breasts. When I looked down, I laughed while I tried to pull
the wet material away so that my nipples would not show
through, although I didn't know why I was doing that since
I was alone in the forest. As I tugged at the blouse, without
knowing why, I looked toward the opposite side of the river
where I saw a man. He was a Lacandón, of that I was certain, yet he was a stranger to me. I stared at him for a long
time. He was garbed in the white tunic of the men of my
tribe, and his hair was cut in the square style worn by Lacandón men. I saw that he was not old yet nor young and that
he looked at me with hunger in his eyes.*

*For a reason unknown to me, I felt my body stiffen as my
feet sunk into the soft bottom soil of the river. I returned the
man's gaze because I found it mysterious, even captivating;
it drew me to him. As I looked at him, he beckoned me to
come to him. His gesture was gentle, not threatening, and all
the while I was filled with a sensation that I had known him
for a long time. I moved toward him although I understood
that regardless of my feelings he was a stranger and that I
should not go near him. Yet, I went to him because all I
knew was that I was answering an impulse that compelled
me to get close to him.*

*When I reached him, he took my hand and led me to
what looked like a nest of green branches. It was cool and
sheltered there; speckled sunlight filtered through the dense
palm fronds and giant mahogany trees. The man was silent
and only the sound of the river's rushing current filled the air*

with its soft splashing. He drew me closer as he lowered him-self onto the nest until I, too, laid by his side. Slowly he removed my blouse and then the rest of my clothing. At no instant did I resist, even when he took off his tunic or when I felt his hands caress my breasts. All the while I was aware that the man's hungry eyes devoured me, that his skin smelled of fresh maize and that his breath was like the fra-grance that lifts from the forest after a rainstorm. When he embraced me, I knew that it was not a man, but a being with the wings of the giant bird that soars above the tallest mahogany trees. I understood this when I felt a cloak of feathers cover me as he mounted and penetrated me. At that moment I surrendered to that birdman.

The ecstasy I experienced was unknown to me. My hus-band, the only man I had ever known, never lifted me to the pinnacles of the forest as did this mysterious stranger. Never had the wind whispered with such feeling as it did now. Never had the river sighed as it was now doing. When my rapture passed I drifted off to sleep, and when I awoke it was nearly dark, but there wasn't a sign of the stranger with whom I had coupled.

I remained there without moving, and I thought of what had happened. Had it been a dream? Had it really taken place? The more I pondered, the more convinced I became that it had been a dream in which I had been visited by a spir-it from the world where my ancestors dwelled. When these thoughts cleared in my mind, I felt a joy I had never before experienced, and I knew that I would submit to that dream no matter how many times it came to me.

I returned countless times to the same place along the river where I first encountered the birdman to repeat the same strange coupling ritual. It happened always in silence, always surrounded by the fragrance of the forest and the sound of the river's rushing cascades. Each time my encounters ended the same way. I fell asleep and awakened believing that it had been a dream sent by the ancestors.

Although part of me was tormented because I heard a voice that told me that what I was doing was forbidden, I abandoned myself to the pleasure I experienced, convinced that it was a dream in which the mysterious birdman was but an instrument of los tatuches. I thought this way until I discovered that I had a child in my belly. When this happened, I again went to the river, but the birdman was not there, and although I waited for hours he did not appear. I returned many times, yet the apparition never again came, leading me to believe that the child I carried was the only reason for our encounters. Now that it was accomplished the wings that had brought the birdman to my side had transported him back to the heights where the gods dwelled. I was left with a child that was part human and part god.

In the meantime, my disappearances into the forest did not remain a secret for long. There were eyes that spied and tongues that wagged. Murmurs filled the air. Village gossips whispered that I had crossed the line into what was forbidden and that each time I went to the river I betrayed my husband. I did not pay attention to those loose tongues because I knew that what had happened to me was reserved only for the blessed. Besides, it was a time when I was no longer a girl, but a woman with a son and two daughters. I knew what I was doing, and what I did belonged not to this world, but elsewhere in the land where gods and los tatuches dwell. So I nurtured the child that grew inside me while I waited for its birth with both joy, but, I admit, some fear.

The River Flows North

The day came when my husband closed the entrance to our palapa, and after that I was ordered to leave the village. It happened without ritual or ceremony because I was deemed unworthy of even that attention. Neither elders nor women gathered to pass judgment. They simply turned their backs on me, certain that I would die of hunger or loneliness once lost in the jungle.

I drifted away in anguish. I had not meant to injure my husband or my children, but I now recognized that I had damaged them. This thought alone caused me deep sadness, but there was nothing I could do to erase what had happened. My people had made the decision to cast me away from them for the rest of my life, and now I was lost as well as vulnerable to any danger that might come my way. What I most longed for were my children, but because I was forbidden to see them, my only source of consolation was in believing that los tatuches had not abandoned me. Knowing this gave me the strength to bring light to the child I carried. I ventured deep into the forest where I built a shelter and fished for food. I wove small trinkets all along and exchanged them for goods in San Cristóbal de las Casas. I also cultivated flowers along the banks of the river that I sold at the cathedral of that city. I did this as I waited the birth of the bird-child, and although I never lost the burden of loneliness, the memory of the mysterious birdman lingered strong inside me.

Months passed until one night I was awakened by a powerful storm. Its thunder shook the earth and frightened me so much that I hid my head in my arms thinking that at any moment a tree would fall on me. The darkness became more horrifying when lightening flashed over and again until it made me think that the trees were in motion, dancing wild-

ly, shaking their branches at me for what I had done. I wailed in fear and loneliness hoping that someone might come to my side to protect me, but no one came. I was alone.

I don't have a recollection of how long the storm lasted. I do remember that whether it was because of my terror or the earth's thunderous vibration, a force suddenly penetrated me and caused me to feel intolerable pain. The throbbing lodged in my belly and dug away at me until I felt the long fingers of the pounding rain rip the child out of my insides. I tried to keep my baby, but it was useless because the small body slipped from between my legs. I knew that the child would be dead. I screamed over and again, calling on the gods to save their creation, but it didn't help. They had become deaf to my pleas.

When I saw that I could do nothing to resist the storm's power, I grasped the small body in an attempt to shelter it from the rain. Then, amid the thunder and lightening, I bit apart its cord and cradled the tiny lump of flesh in my arms while I waited for the storm to run its course. I remained that way until morning light finally cut through the drenched trees and plants.

When there was enough light, I gazed at my mystical child, the gifted messenger from los tatuches, and I saw that it was a man-child. Its form was almost complete; its head, body and limbs were well shaped. I took a long time to look at the child's hands and examine its tiny fingers, almost expecting to find signs that soon feathers would grow from those tips, but no, the boy was ordinary.

I was still in pain when I forced myself to venture out in search of palm fronds in which to wrap my child because I knew what burial I was going to give him. When I gathered what I was looking for, I put the body in one frond layer, rolled and secured it with vines and did that over again, this time with large rocks packed into the shroud.

With the child in my arms, I made my way to the river's edge and there I prayed. Then, holding the baby to my breast, I waded out to the deepest part and I let go. The body floated a short distance and then spun several times until it steadied for a while, then it suddenly plummeted into the depths of the current and disappeared. I remained in the river and thought about the birdman that smelled of maize and about his child, all the while I strained against the same undertow that took him back to his beginnings.

After that I lived the life of an outcast for years during which new waves of children were born into my tribe, growing into youth while they wondered about the identity of the strange woman who roamed the forest. I drifted from village to village and provided for myself from the river, content to speak with strangers with whom I bartered in the city. Although I lived in loneliness, I grew used to being alone because I felt the companionship of los tatuches who did not turn their faces from me after all. Now they repeated their call, saying that I was awaited in the desert, but because I didn't know how to fulfill that calling, I allowed years to slip through my fingers.

Then life in our land changed when the humblest people of our tribes could no longer bear the oppression of los patrones. Like a fever that sprang from the earth, it spread from man to man, woman to woman, until it reached me. I, too, felt the heat that invaded the Lacandona, and I gladly put away my plan to journey to the desert. I listened to the cry of my people who talked openly of how, over the years, los patrones first squeezed us off our ancestral lands into the dense forest and of how we tolerated that injustice for long years until we grew used to life in the forest.

However, that was not enough for los patrones because they wanted more. They discovered that deep in our forest is what they call oro verde, the green gold buried deep in the trunks of the mahogany trees. They desired that wood and went after it, again chasing us in an attempt to drive us from the forest. They cared little that those trees gave us shelter, that they provided cover for our meager plantations, that they protected birds and animals. Our needs, however, meant nothing in the face of so much greed, and los patrones continued to push and to seize, year after year, until our people could no longer tolerate the abuse. It was then that the rebellion was born in Chiapas. It took years to mature, but when the time was ripe, the spirit broke out. It began first with agitation and whispers about uprising and resistance. Then we all heard that the day to overthrow los patrones had come. It happened in our Lacandona villages where new names were whispered: Subcomandante Marcos, Subcomandante Flores and Subcomandante Ramona. We, their followers, became known as Zapatistas, and our army grew larger each day.

People forgot that I was the outcast, and now I was included in all of the rumors and planning. Night after night I returned to my palapa where I put together a fire and reflected on what the future held for me. I didn't know how, or in what manner, yet I was certain that I would be part of what was happening. Yes, I was now old, but I was still strong and I could be of help. I would find the way. My mind turned to the mission los tatuches repeated nearly every night in my dreams. I knew that I had to find the path that would take me to where the brightest star is born and to the land where sand meets the sky. Perhaps the coming revolution would open the way.

I was a living witness to the insurrection that erupted. I was happy because I wanted to be part of that movement, even in a small way, especially when I saw that the rebels were a new breed of men and women. I helped in whatever way I could. I helped construct palapas to house recruits, and I cooked for the soldiers. All of this happened in the heart of the Lacandona jungle, so besides ordinary work I guided recruits, and showed them trails and shortcuts in the forest. After a while, the insurgents forgot that I was a woman nearly sixty years old, and they depended on me as they did on all the other insurgents.

But the movement did not prevail, and in the end it lost valuable ground. During those days of defeat, I shared the sadness that overcame everyone. We had come so close to achieving our goals, but we had been halted; the patrones were too strong, and we too weak. Soon after, people began to scatter, and they helped one another in whatever way possible, but always on the move for fear of retribution.

As these things happened, I saw strangers appear as if from nowhere, but always they kept on the move as they drifted through our villages. At first it was only a trickle of people, many of them who said they came from such distant places as Guatemala and El Salvador. Yet no one settled in our lands. On the contrary, they were in constant movement, always al norte. In time the trickle became a river that flowed north, most of those people headed for the United States.

It was then that I finally saw how I could accomplish my destiny to reach the ancestors in the desert. Like those thousands of uprooted people, I joined them and I became a migrant whose destination never changed. My feet were always planted on a path that pointed north. Sometimes I walked, other times a driver would feel sorry for me, and give me a ride on his truck. Once I was lucky enough to climb onto a cargo train that crept its way from León to Torreón, and it took me closer to my goal. I inched my way slowly from Mexico's southernmost tip up to one of its northernmost posts.

As I made my way north, I witnessed hardship everywhere. I saw more and more people forced to abandon families and homes. Towns became empty. Men, boys and women with bundles on their backs headed north. Whenever I asked why people were leaving, I was told that work was scarce in their part of Mexico and that their children were hungry. What else could be done? Word had it that gringos hired workers on the other side of the border and that the pay was good.

Roads were filled with hopeful people that expected to find a living up there, and I walked alongside them. Sometimes I lingered here and there on my own, but in time I moved on. Throughout my journey I drew attention because I startled people as I appeared from what seemed to them to be nowhere. I know that some pitied me because I was so old, and they helped me in whatever way they could, but others thought I was demented, just another homeless loca, and they mocked me behind my back, but I ignored whatever people thought of me.

Along the way I kept myself alive in different ways. I washed dishes for food stands, or shined shoes in bus depots, or sold Chiclets along roadways, or washed car windows and sometimes I begged. I slept wherever I found shelter and always, when it was time to move on, I planted my feet on the road northward as soon as the sun rose. What kept my heart alive was that I knew that los tatuches waited for me and that I was not alone because the flow of men and women grew each day.

It was the presence of those multitudes that made me pause to think about my own mission and to question why there were so many of them doing what I was doing. I needed to better understand. I contemplated my earliest memories when los tatuches came to me in dreams and called me to them. I saw that I had lived almost all of my life thinking that their voice was only for me, but now that changed because I began to understand that I was not the only one in pursuit of our ancestors' calling. I was not the only one to retrace my people's steps.

I remembered that our ancestors had also migrated ages ago, but at that time their movement was downward from their northern desert world. It was a time when they journeyed south to dwell in the jungles and mountain regions of Mexico, and even farther away, where they have dwelt until this time. Now we, their children, were returning to the place of our ancestors' beginnings. I saw that the river of our lives had reversed its course and that it now flowed back to its original source because it is natural to return to where one begins.

I neared my final destination where I joined a group of migrants on the verge of crossing El Gran Desierto. I did not know their names, but I recognized the expression on their faces. There was sadness because something had uprooted them, yet there was also hope that a new life waited for them. It was a place called La Joyita.

TEN

A Parallel Day Three

A hand cupped over his mouth awakened Leonardo
Cerda, but he didn't move nor did he utter a word.
He knew what was happening when he looked up
and saw the silhouette outlined by moonlight. It was
Armando Guerrero, and when Cerda felt that the hand trem-
bled, he wondered right away about the kind of man he had
cut a special deal for. He saw, too, that Guerrero held a pistol in his other hand.

"Don't make noise because the first one of these *pendejos* that wakes up is dead. You understand me?" Guerrero
whispered into Cerda's ear, so close to his face that *el coyote*
smelled the man's breath. "Get up, grab your rags and let's
get going!"

Cerda cautiously got to his feet without a sound. With
one hand he gathered his backpack and water jug, with the
other he took hold of his boots and then he walked in a

northerly direction. Armando Guerrero followed a few paces behind. He still held the gun with one hand as he lugged his heavy bag with the other one. When he thought they were out of the group's sight, he grabbed Cerda's shoulder, and spun him around to face him.

"I'm in charge now so don't get any funny ideas. I'll blast your guts out if you try anything."

"What's got into you, Guerrero? We made a deal. Remember? I don't like being pushed around, so just calm down."

"Shut up! I'll do whatever I like. Move!"

"Okay! Okay! Just let me put on my boots. I'll last longer with them on."

"All right, put them on, but do it slow and let me see those hands all the time. Remember, I know how to use this thing."

Cerda squatted on the sand and took time to slip into his boots. He was thinking that he hadn't expected this change in Guerrero. When he was ready, he slowly got back on his feet and burned more time as he slapped sand off his rump and legs. He tried to think of what to do.

"I need a smoke."

"Go ahead, but don't think I don't know that all you're doing is killing time. Light that shit and get going!"

Now Cerda felt a certain confusion come over him because Guerrero was not acting like a partner; instead he was treating him like a hostage. Another thing that bothered him was the shaky, nervous way Guerrero handled the gun, making him think that Guerrero really did not know how to handle it.

In the middle of his growing uneasiness, Cerda's mind flashed back to the others he had just abandoned. He knew that more than likely they wouldn't make it without him, so he stopped moving as he tried to think of what to say to Guerrero that might change his mind. The only thing he could think of doing was to turn in different directions as if to get a bearing on where they were. Guerrero, taken by surprise at first gawked at him, but then after Cerda took so long looking in every direction, Guerrero shoved him hard, nearly knocking him off his feet.

"It's daytime so don't give me any shit about not knowing where we're going. C'mon! Let's move!"

"Guerrero, why in the hell are you acting this way?"

"Why? Wasn't it you that took us on that stupid detour to dig up a bunch of bones? Just because that old bag said that she saw some stinking ghost. How do I know you're not going to pull that same shit all over again?"

Cerda shot back, "Didn't we make a deal back there? Didn't I say that I'd get you to Ligurta ahead of the others? As far as I'm concerned a deal is a deal, so drop this *I'm the boss* crap. Besides, what about the detour? What do you care about the goddamn bones, anyway? They're probably not even what the old goat is looking for. Anyway, we're back on track, aren't we? I know that we both see where we're going, but what about the ones we left behind? Aren't you thinking about them?"

"Why should I?" Guerrero snapped.

"Because they'll probably die without my help."

"Goddammit, Cerda! Drop the bleeding heart routine! I don't give a shit about them and neither do you. Don't even try to make me think it's your first time dumping a bunch of losers. Besides, you should've thought of that when you agreed to my proposition. And now you better cough up the extra service."

The River Flows North

Cerda glared at Guerrero because he knew that it wouldn't be the first time he walked away, but the truth was that he was fed up with Guerrero's bellyaching, and he didn't want to go on with him. Yet there was the big bag Guerrero held so close, and that alone made Cerda think hard of what to do next. After a while, he decided to play along and wait for his chance.

"Look, Guerrero, why are you doing this when we're already so close to Ligurta? We don't have to leave anybody behind, I tell you. We can make it together, maybe even today. What're you getting out of leaving them behind?"

"I'm not taking any chances."

"Chances? What are you talking about?" Cerda kept on pressing.

"Of another detour like the one we took for the old bastard and his brat. That was a waste of time. What did we get out of it except a sack of old bones? So, what's next? It'll be that *india* old bag with her pile of shit all over again. *There it is, there it is! The ghost! Let's follow it!*" Guerrero raised his voice, mocking Doña Encarnación. "And you're such a fool, Cerda, that we'll go on another stupid search. Well! We're not going through that crap again!"

"No! That won't happen," Cerda mumbled from behind the stub dangling from his dried out lips.

Without warning, Guerrero jerked up his arm and whipped Cerda's cheek hard with the side of the gun, knocking him down on one knee. "Shut up and start walking. I don't want to hear you again. You think I don't know what you're up to? You're just a shit-eating *coyote* that would slit his own mother's throat for a few coins. You just want to collect more money from that bunch of imbeciles, so just cut the crap!"

Dazed by the blow, Cerda struggled to his feet and again began to head north. He didn't talk; instead he lowered his head and walked without a break to let Guerrero rest. He knew that the man could not deal for long with the heat that intensified each minute. Besides, Cerda had made up his mind and he had a plan. He would take Guerrero off the path, walk him until he dropped and the rest would be easy.

Hours passed while Cerda pushed on until he noticed that the wind had started to blow harder than it ordinarily did at that time of day. After a while he glanced toward the west and saw that the sky looked unusually dark over there. Then it caught his attention that the wind was kicking up tiny dunes all around them; loose branches and twigs skittered by harder and faster. He hadn't planned on those changes, but still he kept on the move, and it wasn't long before he heard Guerrero gasp for breath.

"Hey! Slow down, Cerda. Let's take a break."

Cerda stopped and turned to look at Guerrero. He wasn't surprised to see that his bloated face was ashen with layers of sand and sweat and that his lips were cracked. Guerrero was so stupid that he hadn't even thought of wrapping something around his head to protect himself against the sun's heat. Cerda said nothing, but he did notice that Guerrero no longer pointed the gun at him and that it dangled from his hand, while the other hand seemed welded onto his canvas bag. Cerda saw that this was the chance he was waiting for.

"Look, Guerrero, you're a smart guy. Like I said, why don't I just point you in the right direction and you can make your own way? You don't need me. We can forget about the extra money. Follow the mountains, and in a few hours you'll hit the outskirts of Ligurta."

The River Flows North

"Let you go? Is that what you're saying? Why should I do a stupid thing like that?"

"I already told you! You can make it by yourself, but the others can't. They'll get lost without me. They'll die."

"I don't care what happens to them and neither do you. Goddammit! You and me are going to make it to *la Ocho* and only then can you do what you want. Now, hand me that water jug!"

Cerda gawked at Guerrero and realized for the first time that the man did not have water. When he saw this, Cerda, for the first time, felt frightened for his own life, and instead of handing over the jug, he held it behind his back as a signal that he was not about to give it up. When he spoke, his voice was calm yet edged with determination.

"This water is mine."

"Give me the jug!"

"No!"

"There's enough for the both of us!"

"No!"

"I'll kill you if you don't give me the goddamn thing!"

"No!"

Guerrero's voice became shrill when he saw that Cerda would not relent, so he moved in closer and tried to intimidate him into surrendering the jug, but nothing happened. Cerda would not budge. Guerrero's face became even more bloated with frustration as he glared at *el coyote*. His dilated eyes stared wildly as he tried to focus.

He swayed from side to side as he tried to stabilize himself by spreading his legs, and when he suddenly jerked up the weapon to point at Cerda's face, both men saw that his hand shook. In seconds Guerrero braced his wrist with his free arm trying to get control, but the gun still wobbled. He opened his mouth expecting words to come out, but his tongue only twitched in a silent screech. He tried again, and this time he croaked out what he wanted to say.

"For the last time, give me the jug!"

"No!"

Crazed with thirst and rage, Guerrero pulled the trigger and Cerda dropped flat on his face. Shocked, Guerrero stared at the gun in his wobbling hand, eyes wide open in disbelief of what he had done and he gaped at Cerda's body as if he thought that he would get back on his feet. He stood frozen over the corpse when, as if the gunshot had been a signal, a thunderous clap echoed, and its vibration was so powerful that it knocked Guerrero off his feet. He lifted himself to look in the direction of the roar, and he screamed in terror when he saw a giant wave of sand sweeping toward him.

He rolled over on top of Cerda's body, and he hysterically shook and pummeled the dead man, trying to bring him back. "Get up, Pig! Get up!" he screamed, but he could not hear himself because the wind was blasting without letup, and it pushed him first back, and then forward. Guerrero, eyes nearly shut against the furious sand, instinctively lashed out to find something that might anchor him, but there was nothing except Cerda's body.

In desperation, he grabbed the dead man's belt with both hands hoping that the body's weight would hold him down, but as he clung to it he was horrified to see his canvas bag roll away from him. Guerrero forgot everything, and he let go of the body for a moment. He tried to reach the bag, but he realized that he would be dragged away if he did not regain a hold on the corpse. His instinct to live was stronger than his greed, so he again latched onto the body. The last he saw of his bag was as it ripped into shreds, and scattered the dollar bills in countless directions. The loot that Armando Guerrero had so hungered for and that had driven him to that place of desolation, suddenly disappeared into oblivion.

Now the wind had accelerated to such a pitch that, even as Guerrero clung to Cerda's body, he was dragged with such force that his clothes sheared off, and he screamed in pain as flesh scratched off his arms, shoulders and buttocks. With legs and arms wrapped around Cerda's body, he became nearly fused with the dead man, and both of them rolled first in one direction and than in another until they were slammed against the thick trunk of a saguaro. Guerrero screeched even more when the trunk's long needles jabbed his already raw flesh, but he didn't struggle because the cactus stopped him from being dragged even farther.

Guerrero still clung to Cerda's body, but now he managed to wiggle under it, and he held it against the wind like a shield. He hid his head and face deep under the corpse as he tried to protect his eyes. He stayed there until he heard pitiful screams that were neither human nor animal; the sound was so shrill that it cut through the roar of the wind. Curious to know what cried out with so much pain, Guerrero sheltered his eyes against the wind to take a look, and he caught a glimpse of a tormented coyote dragged by the wind.

The animal, its fur nearly sheared off, rolled over and over as it tried to fight the wind by digging its legs into the sand, but it was useless. In seconds the creature was sucked out of Guerrero's sight, but he heard its terrified yelps long after it disappeared. The screech of the animal horrified him so much that he again buried his head under Cerda's body, and he wept as if he had been a child. He cried until a deadly silence finally fell over the desert; the storm was over.

109

When he realized it, Guerrero tried to free himself from under the dead body, but he saw that his legs were tangled with Cerda's and that his hands were wrapped hard around his belt buckle. He pushed and pulled, but a heavy mound of sand had piled on top of Cerda, adding to the body's weight. Guerrero heaved until he was able to maneuver himself from under the body; only then did he try to climb onto his feet.

First he crawled, and then he lifted himself only to fall first on one knee and then on the other. Guerrero struggled to regain some balance, and he did this while he grunted and cursed until he was finally upright. His lips were bloody, and his mouth was coated with layers of sand that had ground in between his teeth and under his tongue. When he tried to spit out the grime, his palate was so dry that he could not gather enough spittle to rid his mouth of the caking.

When he ran his hand through his hair, he felt it spiked and sticky, and when he touched his face he flinched painfully. He looked down at his clothes and saw that his pant legs were in tatters as were the sleeves of his shirt. Then he swiveled as much as he could to look at his behind. Nearly all of the back part of his trousers had scraped off; his butt was exposed and bloody as were his legs and arms.

When he stood up, he swayed unsteadily, and he tried to pull himself together while his brain cleared. He looked around, but all he made out was gloom; a yellow-gray cloud hung over him, and he couldn't see beyond a few yards. It all looked the same, no matter where he turned. He searched for the mountains, but they had disappeared. He turned in a circle, at first slowly then faster and faster until he became so dizzy that he flopped down on his rear, where he held his head, his mouth agape in a silent scream. Guerrero understood that there was nothing to orient him or to give him a bearing, and he felt his stomach sickening.

When he regained his voice, he screamed for help. He cried out to God and begged for help, but after a while Guerrero's terror turned to rage. He scrambled to his feet, and he cursed everything and everyone in the world. His anger focused on Cerda, and he unleashed his fury on the corpse. He tried to spit on it, kick and stomp it, while he cursed the man for having abandoned him.

Suddenly Guerrero stopped raving. He knew that he was burning what little energy he had left and, even more important, that he was going to die of thirst. He moved away from where he stood, took a few steps first in one direction and then shuffled in another, searching for the jug of water. He thought that maybe it had been dragged along with him and Cerda, but after a while he saw that there was nothing around him but flat sand.

He glared at Cerda's body and again cursed it, but as he stared at the corpse, its face deformed by the bullet that had cracked open its nose and forehead, the memory of the tormented coyote suddenly returned. Guerrero shuddered, convinced that he had to move, otherwise he would die in agony like that animal or he could even end up another stiff with a swollen face, just like Cerda. He looked again because it seemed to him that the mountains had to be on his right. He felt that the sun, although blackened out by the swirl of sand, came through on his left. A feeling was all he had, but because there was nothing else he decided to act on it and get moving.

He plunged headlong as he followed the impression that it was north toward Ligurta. As he moved, he dragged his stiff legs, falling often only to struggle to get back on his feet.

111

All the while he felt that his body was on fire and that his head was on the verge of exploding. His mouth was parched, utterly dry and his lips were so cracked and bleeding that he licked blood with the tip of his tongue, and he savored it as if it had been water. He muttered out loud. He mumbled and spit out curses and accusations. Without realizing it, Guerrero's mind was losing its bearings. His thoughts were mixing, bumping into one another, tangling and not making sense.

Hours passed while he staggered on until he finally saw the outline of houses. Yes! He was positive of what he saw because he made out the big riggers rolling off *la Ocho* onto the truck stop. He could see drivers sitting at a table in the coolness of the air-conditioned café as they waited for a pretty girl to bring those tall cold ones. Guerrero's throat constricted as he sucked his parched tongue because he imagined that thirst-quenching glass of beer. All of it was there in front of him: the town, the café with its refrigerated coolness and its ice-cold beer. With that vision dancing in front of his eyes, he knew that nothing could hold him back now.

Certain that he had reached the outskirts of Ligurta, he ran waving his arms wildly, screaming and laughing hysterically. Although nearly blinded by tears, he saw that he was near a saguaro cactus, and he tried to slow his pace to go around it. As he lunged headlong, Guerrero did not see that his feet were nearly on top of a black writhing mound. Oblivious to everything except his impulse to reach the mirage that beckoned him, he failed to see that the black thing moved, coiled and uncoiled. Suddenly it reared its head and sank its fangs into the calf of his leg. The last thing Guerrero heard before he felt pain shoot up his thigh and into his groin was a loud rattling sound.

The River Flows North

Flat on his back, he screamed in terror. After a while, he dragged himself closer to the saguaro, away from the snake and, as if hypnotized, his eyes were riveted on the creature while it slithered away. The shock of pain brought back some clarity to Guerrero's brain and told him to do something to get rid of the poison. The thought came to him that he should suck it out, so he curled inwardly as he tried to reach the wound, but his spine was too stiff, too hardened. He could not get his mouth that far down his calf although he tried over and again, rolling back and forth on the sand.

In panic, he pressed his fingers against the pronged wound and tried to squeeze or claw out the poison, but as he struggled he saw the bloat invade first his calf, then creep upward toward his thigh, and then onto his entire body. It took a while before he felt his chest constrict, forcing him to gasp, mouth wide open, in an attempt to suck in air. He struggled, but it was no use because in a matter of minutes his lungs gave out.

Armando Guerrero did not realize it, but he died just on the other side of the same saguaro cactus that sheltered Cerda's body. He had trekked hours convinced that he had reached Ligurta, but he had unknowingly gone a full circle and returned to the place where he had abandoned Leonardo Cerda, *el coyote*, who could have saved him.

ELEVEN

Leonardo Cerda

W*as I tejano or mexicano? I never really made up my mind because ever since I can remember, my mother and father crossed over between Laredo on the Texas side and Nuevo Laredo in Mexico like it was the same town. I had family on both sides of the Río Grande, cousins, aunts, uncles and even a couple of abuelos. I spoke English and Spanish, but most of the time I didn't even know how I was talking. It all came pretty natural to me.*

I was born on the Texas side of the Río Grande in 1938 during the time when almost everybody was out of a job, but my family was big, and everybody stuck together working as piscadores, harvesters of fruit and vegetables. We did okay when the seasons were fat and work was all over the place, but when times got really bad, the family stuck even closer

114

together and shared whatever we had. That way we made it through the rough days.

I had a good life even if I worked the fields ever since I can remember. I went to school only when there wasn't enough work, and when I was out in the fields, I didn't miss school because I thought that sticking my nose in books was silly. I didn't like those stuffy classrooms where I hardly ever had enough time to get to know any of the other kids. Besides, they were almost all a bunch of gabachos.

I was born between my brothers and sisters; the two guys were older and the girls smaller and I can't explain it, but I always felt separated. I didn't belong with the two boys, and I didn't fit in with the girls. This made me a loner from the beginning, but I didn't mind being on my own. I even liked it.

On top of that, the way I looked made me different. Compared to my brothers who were round, chubby and on the short side, I was tall, skinny and long-boned, and this gave me a lanky look that made people make fun of me because I looked freaky. This didn't bother me either. Instead, I used it to clown around to make others laugh, and this made me popular with just about everybody.

I know that it was this lone wolf thing that made me feel close to my mother. Now that I think of it, it was probably because she was skinny and lanky too, just like me. By the time I was a teenager I had gotten real close to her and loved her more than anyone else. I confess that I adored everything about her. I loved the way she talked and combed her hair; the way she walked high on the balls of her feet, and I was even crazy about the long front teeth that stuck out just a little from under her upper lip.

I had the same teeth, only on me they got so long they were what everybody called genuine buckteeth. But there was more to what I felt about her than just her looks. The truth is that we were both real crazy. We used to laugh like hyenas at just about anything, and we had a lot of fun imitating other people. It just came natural to us, I mean the way we could walk and talk just like Tío Lalo or Doña Berta. Whenever mom and me got together, no matter where, the room always broke out into big old belly laughs when we pulled one stunt after another. Now I know that it was this craziness that tied me so tight to her.

Our favorite place to do our thing was the kitchen where we mimicked famous people like Pedro Infante and Jorge Negrete. At those times, anyone who hung around the house packed into the kitchen just to get in on the fun because they knew that room was the best part of our house. My mom did a great Lucha Reyes and when she belted out those ranchera songs, everyone shouted, Do it again! Do it again! But our best imitations were of family and friends, and we got so close to the mark that those who watched us doubled over in fits, while those that were the ones we poked fun at looked all bent out of shape because they didn't know if they should laugh or gripe.

We loved to go through those routines. No matter what we did we always ended up slapping our thighs or each other on the back because it was all so damn funny. It never failed that some neighbor would walk by outside the kitchen window, and he'd catch the howling that bubbled out through the screen. Right away the guy would know that somebody was getting razzed, and it made him wonder if this time it was him. Sure enough, that poor guy wouldn't be able to hold back, and he'd shout right into the window. Señora Cerda, is it me you and your son are making fun of?

116

The River Flows North

We couldn't answer right away because we had a hand slapped tight over our mouths. We'd just keep real quiet until old Don Cuco, or whoever it was, made it to the other side of the street, and then we'd break out louder than ever. We'd snort and honk all over the place. The shrieks we let out filled the house with a racket that could be heard all the way down the street to the corner.

But our life changed. As it turned out, a really bad thing suddenly hit us, and all of it came at one time when I was around sixteen. With just a few months in between, my two brothers died, one in a tractor accident, the other of a mysterious fever, and from that time onward, all the laughter disappeared. Our kitchen got dark and quiet.

I've always hated dawn because it was at daybreak when the bad news first slithered into my family's heart. First came the knock on the front door, and then I heard my father's muffled voice; pretty soon that was drowned out by my mother's moans. Whoever was at the door brought news to say that a tractor in the fields near Corpus Christi had crushed my older brother.

My brother's death, funeral and burial were the first sad memories in my life, and I've never forgotten any part of it, especially my mother's grief. I couldn't understand how someone filled with so much laughter could change into the crying, wailing woman that was now my mother. I tried to comfort her, but I got nowhere. Nothing could take away her pain. That is, until a new heartache came to take its place.

My second brother started with big-time bellyaches a few weeks afterward. At first, no one paid attention because everybody knew he was the big eater of the family. He was the one with a mule's stomach that nothing could hurt, but when he complained of pain and that he couldn't stop going

117

to the toilet, then my mother started to worry. She brewed
him teas, but when that didn't work the old barrio comadres
came up with other treatments.

We tried everything, but no matter how much we made
up different brews and rubdowns, nothing worked. He sunk
deeper into the mysterious shit that ate him up little by little.
My mother was desperate to find a cure for her son, so she
brought in Doña Milagros, a healer, hoping the old curandera
could save him, but no luck. The fever stuck and wouldn't go
away. My brother died even with the healer's rubbings, con-
coctions and secret prayers.

Although she struck out with my brother, I never forgot.
She was a skinny little thing decked out in a long black dress,
and she always had a raggedy black rebozo wrapped around
her head. What's stuck with me the most after all these years
is how she smelled of añil mixed with olive oil. I remembered her all over again when I faced Doña Encarnación just
the other day.

After the death of my brothers, nobody was sadder than
my mother. But I wasn't free either because now something
hit me right in the face when I saw that I wasn't the middle
kid anymore; now I was the oldest. Goddamn! In a way that
I've never been able to explain, this sucked something out of
me, and it made me understand that I couldn't be the clown
anymore, that I couldn't laugh with my mother like we used
to before all that bad luck snuck into our house. I didn't like
it, but that's the way things turned out, and from that time
on I clammed up. I was gloomy and shit-faced most times.

Not much time passed before my father tried to shake my
mother from all that sadness; he sold our house and moved
her and the girls to the other side of the border. They settled

in Nuevo Laredo where familia tried to give them just a little bit of happiness.

I knew that everybody thought that I was going to join the move south, but I decided to go out on my own since I didn't want to live in Mexico where I felt strange, pretty much an outsider. The only person that could've made me want to stay was my mother, but she was buried in sadness. She was somewhere else; she hardly even recognized me and, to tell the truth, I couldn't stand it. So on the day everybody headed south, I packed up and set off to drift in and out of cotton fields. I tramped all those roads that no one knows about, and I hitchhiked or hopped on trains, and I lived like a hobo for a long time.

I didn't mind being a drifter. In fact, I liked being on my own, on the loose and, most of all, I liked the time I had to myself even when I hung around other bums who were alone and shiftless just like me. I got to know a bunch of lonely, ragged guys while I drifted from one side of Texas to the other. I boozed on cheap wine and ate whatever I could scrounge up. Nobody asked me who I was, or where I was from. Whenever a bunch of us came together around a campfire, we laughed, sometimes bawled like babies, but most of the time we cussed up a storm while we told all kinds of bullshit stories.

As time passed, I became a nomad while I moved through Texas up to Amarillo, then down and west to El Paso. From there I turned east to Waco and Beaumont until I got to the water's edge in Galveston. After that I made a U-turn and started my trip in reverse. I did the whole thing more times than I can count, and I hardly kept track of small towns and truck stops that I passed. I slept off highways and under bridges. If the season was right I worked a harvest picking and packing, but whenever I made a few extra bucks I hit the honky-tonks and got loaded. Christ! It was in one of those drunks that some wise guy punched out my front teeth. It hurt a lot, but I didn't care and like always, I moved on as soon as I could. I didn't like to stay too long in one place.

I was a real asshole, but not all of the time because I didn't forget my familia while I was free and easy. I dropped post-cards into corner mailboxes at least three times a year. I crammed those cards with messages for my little sisters and father, but especially for my mother. I thought of returning home for a visit, but whenever that idea hit me I shoved it back in my mind because I was scared to see mom's sad face. I admit that I didn't want to see her that way. What I really wanted was to remember her and me when we clowned around in our old kitchen.

But the day came when I had enough of the drifter stuff. I needed to see my mother and the rest of the gang, so without writing to tell anybody of my plan, one day I went back to Nuevo Laredo and just walked up to the front door of the house. When I knocked at the rickety screen door, no one came so I let myself into the front room where I found my old man sitting in a worn-out easy chair; he was dozing in front of a turned off television. Real quiet, I took a chair and sat down to look at him. I was surprised to see how hunched over and wrinkled he had gotten since I last saw him. More than ten years had gone by.

I stared at him from his scalp down to his feet stuffed into old beat-up chanclas. He wasn't big and strong like I remem-bered him. He was now a skinny old man, and his big mop of wavy hair had turned into scraggly puffs of thin hair. His face was covered with wrinkles and dark blobs; his jaw hung open letting me see gums without teeth. I took a long time to

*look at his hands and remembered how they used to be pow-
erful and how they worked so hard when he picked fruit and
packed crates. Now his fingers were all swollen and crooked
at the knuckles.*

*Shit! I don't know what came over me, but I wanted to
get down on my knees, take my old man in my arms and tell
him how much I loved him and how bad I felt because I
went away for so many years. But instead I just sat there letting my eyes fill up with tears until I cried like a goddamn
baby. I didn't even try to hold back what I felt. What the hell!
There was no one there to see that I was bawling.*

*I don't know how much time had passed when I sudden-
ly saw that my father had opened his eyes and was staring at
me. Jesus! His eyes were young, filled with light and he
looked at me like when I was just a kid. We sat in front of
each other like the years had stood still, like I was still the little clown shit, and he was the big rugged piscador of his
young days. After a while, I slid off the chair and kneeled
real close to him, and we wrapped our arms around each
other for a long time.*

*I took hold of my old man's arm to help him out of the
chair, and as I did this I knew that I was going to ask about
my mother, but I was afraid of what he would say. When we
made it into the kitchen, I realized my amá was no longer
around. The room was dark and there weren't any of the
things amá used to have in her favorite place. I sniffed the
air, but I didn't pick up any of her great aromas, and there
weren't any jars or pots or plates filled with her spices and
sauces. I looked around and hoped to see strands of garlic
and red chilies hanging by the stove, but there was nothing.
The only things lined up on the sink counter were small yellow containers of medicine.*

Graciela Limón

When I asked him why she died he said that tristeza had killed her. She couldn't stop being sad after the boys died. That's when she really left because all she did after that was sit in a chair and look out the window. Her body was left behind, but not her ánima. It left with the boys.

After that I stayed in my father's house for years, by day I would cross the border into Texas where I worked in the picking fields or in construction. At the end of the day, I would cross back to Nuevo Laredo where I would get together with my father on el porche to drink a couple of beers and watch the sun go down while we told each other stories. My old man would tell about the days when he worked in the fields, and I would talk about my adventures on the road; afterward we would eat whatever I fixed. Over the years, whenever I looked back on my life, I saw this time as almost the best of my life.

During those quiet years, I was pretty much a changed man. I married a girl named Natalia Urrutia, and I was happy with my new life even when it hit me that now I had to be tied down to one place. I thought a lot about this because the old hit-the-road bug came back. I really felt the itch just like in the old days, but now that I was married it slammed into me that my life would be just like everybody else's, that I was expected to stay put.

Not long after I married my father died; that day all the familia came over with food and drinks. When we walked to the cemetery to bury him, a couple of the cousins who were musicians played "Las Golondrinas," making everybody cry like babies. I looked around and thought that I had never seen so many people dressed in black and that we must've looked like a bunch of crows.

122

The River Flows North

When we got back to the house, the prayers kicked in. Damn! There were so many rosaries going at the same time that the Ave Marías flew wall to wall. In the middle of all the sighs and mumbles my sisters and I got so drunk that we cried ourselves silly, but everybody understood because it's not every day that a father dies.

After my father's death the house felt empty, and I can't explain how much I missed him. I went and came across the border to work, but things were stiff between Natalia and me. Maybe it was because she was a lot younger than me, or maybe it was because the itch to hit the road kept getting deeper and bigger inside me.

A year passed and we had twin girls. They were cute, and I was real crazy about them, but my road fever wouldn't go away. I started to get crabby and nasty, but worse of all I got jealous, real jealous, about what Natalia did when I was at work across the border. First I imagined that as soon as I took off to work some son of a bitch slithered into my house and went straight into my bed where the two of them fucked up a storm. I tried to wipe out those pictures from my brain, especially when I came back home at night when I tried to be nice and cheery, just like nothing bad had gone through my head. The bad thing was that as the days and months went by the jealousy and the hit-the-road fever got worse.

After a while I convinced myself that it wasn't my imagination because I was sure that she was really screwing around. I didn't have any proof, but what the hell, I didn't need any, so the day came when I couldn't take it anymore. Without a word I left for work one morning and never went back home. I didn't give a shit that I was leaving Natalia and the girls on their own. All I knew was that I wasn't going to be tied down anymore. What I really wanted was to hit the road again; to hitch a ride on some pickup and head in whatever direction that road took me. I admit I wasn't the marrying kind. It had been a big mistake for me. So I walked away, and never stopped moving.

I headed north across the border to make my way up to San Antonio, and from there west as far away from Texas as I could get, all the way to the Pacific coast in California. When I finally got there, I drifted down close to the border where I took a job on a San Ysidro dairy farm. It was there that I started to see that something different was happening. Little by little I saw that things were changing big time and that people couldn't just come and go across the line like before. I kept my ears open to hear stories of raids and how people were scared to get caught. There was a lot of talk about coyotes, and that really grabbed my attention because right away I sniffed out a chance to make money just for doing what came natural to me.

I knew the lay of the land on both sides, and I spoke the right way. When I was on the gabacho side people thought I was a tejano, and a mexicano when I was in Mexico. So what if a goddamn coyote is nothing but a scumbag? Somebody's gotta do the job. Right? So I made my way across the border to Mesa Otay where I spent a long time mixing in with the crowds, and I got ready to make the crossing. It happened every night, and in the beginning I only watched, kept my ears open, planned and asked questions. After that I got to work.

Later on when the patrols got real tough in California, the action shifted over to the Arizona desert so I followed, and just like I did when I was in California, I went out into the goddamn desert more times than I remember before I felt ready. I took a long time to check out the desert in its crazy moods and screwy swings, in its different seasons and its times of day and moon changes. I memorized the lay of the terrain, the location of old water holes and the shortest routes that connect Mexican truck stops to Interstate 8. In time, I got to be one of the best.

All I thought of was that I would get money for doing what I did best. I was a crazy lone wolf, and that was all there was to it. It didn t bother me that the migrants didn't have legal papers, because for me the border was only a big invention anyway. After that, if they got caught, well, they got caught; I took their money anyway. Sometimes I lied to them, and lots of times I walked out on them.

After I got to work on the coyote thing, I never stopped until now that a bullet did the job, and all because I decided to lead that bunch of dreamers on a little detour. The kid wanting to find what was left of his amá got to me. Christ! I would have gone into any goddamn desert to dig holes all the way down to Hell for one of my amá's bones.

TWELVE

Day Four

Leonardo Cerda was on their minds so they cursed him, convinced that he could have saved them. Now what was left of the group sat huddled in a circle; they crouched so close to one another that their knees nearly touched. Menda held her head in her hands; Celia clasped her arms around her knees; Borrego squatted rigidly with his eyes half-closed while his brother Nicanor stared into empty space. His face was expressionless and stiff.

The morning after the sandstorm dawned gloomy with the air still loaded with residue sand. When they opened their eyes, all they could think of was that they were hopelessly lost except for the now visible blurred silhouette of the mountains. Along with the thought of Leonardo Cerda, their heads swirled with the certainty of death. They were thirsty and hungry; what was left of their clothes barely protected

126

them against the relentless sun and wind. After a while it was Menda who forced herself out of that trance.

"Look! There are the mountains! Now we know in what direction to go. C'mon! We're close to Ligurta. We're almost there!"

They silently forced themselves to their feet, except Nicanor who was trapped in a stupor. He stared ahead, eyes blank until his brother took hold of his shoulders and yanked him up to his feet. One by one, Celia, Borrego and finally Nicanor tried to shake off the listlessness that oppressed them. With Menda at the head, they followed.

They moved like zombies, legs heavy and stiff as they struggled to maneuver their feet along the treacherous sand drifts. No one spoke; only a few moans escaped from somewhere deep inside them. When Menda looked back to assure herself that they followed, she was frightened by those distorted, bloated faces. Their cracked, bleeding lips were the only sign that they were still alive. She knew that she looked like them, or maybe even worse, because she felt that her face was about to explode. When she put her fingers to her lips she felt the swelling, so she dropped her hand because it pained her too much, but despite her stiffened tongue she forced herself to speak.

"Just a little bit more, *compañeros*! Remember that we're already on this side of the line. We're where we want to be! Just a few more *kilómetros*, maybe one or two, and we're right where all the good work waits for us. Just think! We'll be able to write home and tell everyone how we survived. All we have to do is try just a little bit more! Please! Try!"

Menda talked as she struggled to give her companions confidence although she, too, was close to losing hope. She was afraid that they were losing the will to continue, but she made up her mind that she would not let them give up, and this determination injected her with a fresh dose of energy despite the haze that had invaded her mind. In that muddle she became convinced that Doña Encarnación's spirit beckoned her, waving her arms and showing her the way.

The old woman's apparition inspired Menda to keep her companions on the move even if it was only a few feet at a time. If it was not Borrego or Nicanor, it was Celia, who fell or stumbled or came to a halt, paralyzed and unable to go forward. Still, with her eyes constantly on Doña Encarnación's murky silhouette, Menda did not give up urging her companions to keep on the move, to not give up. "C'mon, we're almost there!"

In a while she stopped to give the others a chance to catch up, but at that moment a gust of wind blew hard, and it made her wince with fear of another storm. She steadied herself, tense and ready for what might come next, but she was relieved to see that it was nothing; just a brief flurry. Menda peered ahead and noticed that the quick burst of wind had cleared the air and that it gave her better visibility of what was up front.

Then, as happens when dense fog shifts, when it suddenly exposes hidden objects, a silhouette appeared. At first, Menda thought it looked like a boat that floated just above the sand, so she blinked several times, convinced that what she saw was in her imagination, but the image only became clearer, closer to her. She stared at it for a minute before she let out a yelp she didn't think was left in her.

By this time the others had come close and they, too, stood rigid, gripped by what was in front of them. It was not a hallucination; they all saw it. As if by magic, each one forgot the pain, fatigue and thirst that had been grinding them into the sand, making movement nearly impossible, forcing them to grovel and crawl. Now they stood, mouth hanging open, swollen eyelids struggling to open wider to take in the thing that shimmered in the desert sun, nearly fooling their eyes into believing that it was floating.

Nicanor was the first to react, "It's a phantom!"

"No!" Borrego countered. "It's real. We all see it! I think it's a boat!"

"What's a boat doing in the middle of the desert?" Celia countered what Borrego said.

Finally convinced that it wasn't an apparition, Nicanor saw the thing for what it was. "It's not a boat! It's a truck!"

After that Borrego shouted, "Shit! That's what it is!"

When the reality of what they saw sank in, they moved toward the truck, at first cautiously as if expecting something vicious to lunge out from behind or from under the vehicle. When they got close enough they saw that it was turned on its side, its top badly crushed and its sides scraped and dented. The passenger door had been ripped off, and the truck's undercarriage was exposed, clogged with sand and debris.

They circled the truck slowly, sometimes touching a tire, sometimes placing the flat of a hand on a side panel. Borrego inched up to it and flattened an ear against the back panel as he listened, trying to make out movement. At the same time Menda made her way close enough to peer into the front. She expected to find a body at the wheel, but there was nothing.

Sure that there was nothing going on inside, they moved over to squat against the truck. They were quiet for a while; not much talk was needed. They knew about vehicles that transported people along with the promise to drop them off in cities deep inside the country. Not only that, they had all heard the ugly stories that filtered all the way back home, and, because of that, each one of them had been warned against an attempt to reach the United States that way. Nonetheless, they were shocked to actually encounter one of those feared trucks.

Almost at once questions slipped out as each one jabbered, their voices overlapped and tripped on each other. No one knew who said what, and they answered each other without understanding what they said.

"*¡Dios mío!* How did it get here?"

"Maybe somebody drove it across the desert."

"Maybe. But there isn't a road. How could that be done?"

"These vehicles have special tires. Like the ones the *gringo Migra* drives."

"No! I think the storm blew so hard it rolled it all the way here."

"That's possible, but what about the driver?"

"He was probably killed in the storm. The truck rolled over, maybe a lot of times. Anybody can see that."

"Or maybe he just abandoned it. Ran away like a stinking traitor"

"Probably."

In the end it was Menda and Borrego that speculated about the driver and how the truck ended up in that part of the desert. Now and then Celia and Nicanor put in a word, but after a while they mostly listened to the other two companions. In a few minutes they all fell into silence. They all thought the same thing, but were afraid to come out with what was on their minds.

"We have to look inside," Menda's voice was firm.

"I don't know," Borrego looked at her. "What if we find dead people?"

"All the more reason for us to look." She stared at the others to see what they thought.

"But what will we do if we find bodies?" Nicanor asked.

"We have to look anyway!" Menda now sounded even more certain.

Borrego, afraid of what they might find, disputed Menda, "But what if we had never seen this van? It would just stay here forever. Right? We can think of it that way."

"We have to look, I say!" Her voice finally prevailed over the objections of the others who were terrified of what they would discover once the rear of the van was opened. Without another word, she got to her feet and moved close enough to grab onto the handle of the rear door closest to the ground. She wrapped her hands around the lever, and she yanked, but her strength was so depleted and the door so clogged with sand that it remained unmoved. She tried again, but failed a second time.

By now the others were behind her to take a turn yanking the thing open. First Borrego tried, then Nicanor, then Celia, but it was useless because, although the handle turned, its inner mechanism was frozen shut. This gave the others a chance to again argue against Menda.

First it was Nicanor, "You see? It's a sign that we should keep out."

Then Borrego followed, "C'mon! This isn't our business! Let's just keep moving! We're wasting time!"

Celia jumped in, "We're only looking for more trouble. We've got enough of our own. We're so weak we can hardly stand."

By this time they had circled Menda and scowled in her face, determined not to look inside the vehicle; however, she did not budge, and she glared back into their terrified eyes.

131

She knew what they felt because she was just as frightened, but she could not walk away from what she believed was a deadly cargo. "And what if it was us inside that van?"

Nicanor snapped, "But it isn't us, Menda! And even if it was, we would all be dead, wouldn't we? We wouldn't care."

"Look at it another way, Nicanor. What if someone came to find that here was Borrego and his brother, and one day that person would write to their family to tell them where their life ended. Maybe they would tell how a small prayer was said and that they were buried like human beings, not abandoned like dried-out jackals."

Menda's words broke the tension, and after a while the three that refused to open the door began to look around in search of something to pry the thing open. It was Nicanor who slithered up into the front cab, and after rummaging through debris, he found a tire wrench under the driver's seat. He came round to pick at the door's lock with the tool, and it wasn't long before they heard the mechanism snap. After that they knew all they had to do was pull on the door. Yet, they hesitated until Menda again urged them to move. "C'mon, we'll do it together."

The panel popped open. Daylight flooded the van's bed revealing a ghastly scene. The four were too worn-out to let out howls or screams; only puny moans escaped their parched throats. Celia fell on her knees, and Nicanor turned away, unable to take in what he saw, and he began to gag, mouth wide open. Menda and Borrego stared in disbelief at what was in the van.

Because the vehicle had landed on its side bodies were crammed to one side, piled one on top of the other. The ones on the bottom were wedged into the crack between the side and floor of the cabin. At first it was nearly impossible to tell how many corpses were there because they were tangled, and all that could be made out were legs entwined with arms; heads dangled grotesquely under and over torsos. Those bodies were desiccated, but not yet skeletons. What used to be faces were now skulls covered by blackened, dried-out skin, teeth protruded in a horrified grin.

It was obvious that the victims, all of them naked, had ripped off their clothes in an attempt to lower their body heat. A closer look showed that there were several men and some women, one still gripping the body of a child. The inside panels of the van were covered with bloody scratches telling of a desperate, futile attempt to cut through the metal to let air into that deadly trap.

"*¡Dios nos libre!*"

"*¡Madre mía!*"

Menda and Borrego muttered whatever words filtered through their shocked brain. The other two were on their knees. Celia moaned inconsolably, and Nicanor was in a half faint. Anxiety gripped Menda, and her breathing became irregular; when she felt that she was going to faint she threw herself on the sand. Borrego got on his knees next to her and cradled her head on his lap. After a while he whispered, "Menda, this happened a long time ago. I think they were trapped in this van weeks ago, maybe even months. We couldn't have helped them."

"I know! I know!" Menda's voice was muffled. "Still, it's so awful! What torment they must have suffered."

"I think the van was abandoned somewhere in the desert, then dragged to this place by the storm." Borrego tried hard to comfort her, but he felt that his words could not help. After that he was quiet for a long time, his ears alert because he expected to hear moans and screams begging for help, as if the van was still filled with the echoes of unspeakable terror and pain. In a while he spoke up again. "Menda, what are we going to do? We can't bury them. We don't have a way to do it, and we're just too weak. We can't."

"I know, but we have to do something. Come! Let's go to your brother and Celia. Maybe between the four of us we can think of what to do."

The four crawled to the side opposite the van's open door where they huddled, trying to calm themselves enough to think of what to do. They saw the obvious right away. They could not bury the bodies, yet they felt they should do something, and it was this part that forced them to think and talk. Finally Celia suggested that the vehicle could be considered a tomb if they shut it up again to protect the remains from prowling animals.

"That's the answer. But is that all we're going to do?" Menda thought they should do more.

"What if we try to find their papers?" Borrego tried to answer the question. "Maybe when we get to Ligurta we can contact their families back home."

At first, his idea struck them as the right thing to do; yet they weren't sure, so no one said anything. A moment later Celia came up with another thought. "I don't think that will work, but what if we take some of their clothes? We're in rags, and I think they'd like us to protect ourselves with their things." The thought of putting on dead people's clothes made the other three shiver; speechless, they gawked at Celia. She understood and, without a word, lowered her head.

Borrego had another idea. "Why don't we untangle the bodies and place them side by side to give them a little dignity. Then we should cover them up with the clothes."

The River Flows North

They all agreed. "Let's do it."

Although horrified at what they were about to do, they approached the bodies but did not realize that stiffness had by now welded those arms, legs and torsos one to the other. They soon found out, however, when Borrego and Nicanor tried to separate a man that had fallen on top of another one. The fusion was so complete that only by breaking bones could the corpses be separated. When they saw what had happened, they gave up the idea, backed away and in silence closed the panel door as securely as possible. Before leaving the site, one of them traced the sign of the cross on the heavy layer of sand encrusted on the van's siding.

"There's still light in the sky. Let's walk more."

Menda again took up her position and started to make her way toward *la Ocho*. Still in deep shock, the other three followed, and she moved ahead until she looked back to see that they had fallen behind. She paused to catch her breath while she took time trying to erase the images of crumpled, dried-out bodies that blocked her vision, but no matter how much she shook her head, the ugly pictures would not go away. She retraced her steps to find Borrego crumpled over as he held Nicanor in his arms. Both sobbed. Celia had fallen on her knees dry heaving; her body convulsed with retching. Menda, utterly exhausted, fell by her side, and she put her arms around the young woman trying to comfort her, but she saw that Celia was inconsolable. Menda turned and crawled over to the brothers.

Borrego put his lips to Menda's ear and whispered, "I saw him drink his own piss. That's why he's acting so bad. I think he's going crazy."

"How could he do that?" Menda spoke in disbelief.

"Look! He found this jug somewhere back there and pissed in it, and then he drank it."

"*¡Dios mío!* What's happening to us? Borrego, don't let him do it again, and don't think of doing it yourself."

"Menda, I'm so thirsty. I can't think of anything else."

"I'm dying of thirst, too, but I'm thinking of getting to *la Ocho*. That makes me forget that I'm so thirsty."

"I don't think we'll ever make it to that *pinche* road. Menda, we're going to die out here like stinking burros, just like those people in the van."

"No! We're going to live. I promise you. We're going to live! Look, let's rest a little and you'll see, we'll feel better in a while. Try to sleep. Put your arms around your brother. Comfort him."

Menda, on all fours, crawled back to Celia and saw that her eyes were closed, but she didn't know if the woman was asleep or if she had fainted. She didn't try to wake her. Instead she cradled her in her arms while she thought of her children. Menda, too, drifted off, defeated by pain caused by the heat, an intolerable thirst that slowly closed off her throat and images of twisted bodies that were now seared into her brain.

Suddenly Borrego's screams shook Menda back into consciousness, but she didn't know if she had drifted off for hours or perhaps only minutes. What she did see was that it was still daylight and that Borrego was on his knees, so close to her face that his nose almost rubbed her cheek. It took her a few seconds to understand why he was hysterical.

"He's gone!"

"What?"

"My brother! He's gone! Look! His footsteps! That's all that's left! We have to follow him! We have to find him!"

The River Flows North

Menda was so confused that she had difficulty understanding what was happening. She finally understood that Nicanor was gone, but she knew that they did not have the strength to run after him. She took hold of Borrego's shoulders and tried to calm him, but he only screamed louder for his brother, yet she knew that she had to do something before he lost his mind. "We'll go, Borrego, but first help me with Celia. She can't move on her own."

"Leave her! She's almost dead."

"No! Help me with her or I'm not moving from here."

Borrego, intimidated by Menda's threat, yanked Celia's arm, linking it over his neck. Menda did the same. Together they hoisted the woman and dragged her forward as her legs dangled; her limp feet cut deep rows into the treacherous sand. Their own footprints were black holes that would soon disappear into the wind.

Menda and Borrego hauled Celia until they could go no farther, and at that point they dropped, overwhelmed by fatigue. In a mound, the three clung to one another too tired to speak; hardly able to keep their eyelids open while night enveloped them. Overcome by exhaustion, they drifted on a wave of delirium, where they imagined themselves free of the pangs of thirst and the terror of death. Celia fell deeper into the oblivion of hallucination where she saw herself by the river embankment together with her husband and daughter.

137

THIRTEEN

Celia Vega

*E*very woman has her story. I have mine, and, in a
way, it's a love story, but in another it isn't. It all
begins in the state of Hidalgo in a town called
Venta Prieta. Most of all my story has to do with
Zacarías Tiburcio who, like me, was a native of those parts.
I can't remember when we became playmates. Maybe it
began when his father first came to my home to tend to the
garden. I think that's when Zacarías and I became insepara-
ble, and we spent whatever time we had playing and swim-
ming in the river. Whenever our friendship began isn't
important to me because what matters is that he became a
part of my life from the beginning and that it was natural for
us to one day become lovers.

Zacarías never talked about his mother or father so his
beginnings were a mystery to me, but one thing was certain,
and that was that his ancestors had inhabited the land cen-

turies before mine. For my part, I don't know when the Vegas migrated into that part of Mexico, but it was much after the original people. What I do know is that my family prospered in lands and servants, and that it was people like us who were served by people like the Tiburcios. By the time Zacarías and I were born, our families were locked into those who were above and those who were below.

We would still meet by the river to swim at the age of eighteen. That is, until the day when what had been childish fun became a powerful attraction that led us to what was forbidden. I suppose I should have seen that it was inevitable, but when it happened it took us by surprise, without warning. On that special day, we had just come out of the river when an irresistible urge suddenly took hold of us. Before we knew what was happening, Zacarías was on top of me, caressing and kissing me. I surrendered. It momentarily hurt, but then I felt pleasure overtake me while the ground shook so violently that I clung to him, afraid to be thrown off the earth into empty space.

It happened fast, and we wanted more, so we did it again. When it was over, we leaned against one another in silence, afraid of what we had done because we knew that it was forbidden. That day was the first of the many times that Zacarías and I coupled, and our love grew more intense with each encounter. We did it until I realized that I was pregnant. I admit I understood the seriousness of what happened. Not only was I carrying a child outside of marriage, but I had also coupled with un indio. I knew that I had defied what I learned from my beginnings.

During the first months of my pregnancy, while I could still hide it from prying eyes, I experienced indescribable anxiety. What would my family do to me? More important than this fear was the thought of Zacarías because I was afraid for him. What would my family do to him? No one can imagine how I longed for someone to turn for help, but I had no one. I couldn't go to my mother, or an aunt or teacher or older sister because I knew they would not understand what I had done. They would not see that the baby I carried was because of my love for Zacarías. I found myself alone, and I became depressed, distant. I lost sleep, and I hardly ate.

Zacarías didn't turn his back on me. He begged me to allow him to approach my father to tell him that he intended to marry me, but I stopped him because I was convinced that it would put him in danger. Instead I allowed time to pass while my terror grew, all the while I felt paralyzed and powerless to do anything. I tried to hide my sadness from my father for as long as possible, but it was useless because in time his eyes told him everything. When he discovered my condition, he threw me out of his house, not because of my pregnancy but because the father of my child was Indio, and poor. It happened just as I had feared.

This is where my love story ends. Now let me begin the real one, the one that put me on this road of sighs. After I was thrown out of my family home I lived with Zacarías and his family while we waited for our child Adina. We didn't marry although we knew that others considered that what we were doing was wrong. That didn't matter to us because no one knew how much we loved each other, and we couldn't see it as something bad. I tried to reconcile with my family, not for the comforts they could give us, but because I thought they would want to be part of Adina's life, but no, the door was shut tight against me. It was as if I had never existed, and they were cruel as well, making sure that no matter where I went, gossiping tongues were there first.

Well, those people received their own punishment because in time, like a distorted reflection of Zacarías's and my own life, everything in our town began to crumble. The decline took years, but it was steady and it hit everybody. It was a time when jobs were lost; life as people had known it disappeared. Zacarías's father eventually lost all of his garden work; not even the public parks had jobs for him. Zacarías tried everything from working in car garages to collecting trash, but although he landed some work, it usually ended after a short while. He went out to the surrounding ranchos hoping to find work only to find that dozens of men and women were standing on line in front of him.

I tried to find work. I left my little girl with her grandmother, and I went out in search of work cleaning houses, serving tables in restaurants, even washing and combing hair in salons, but I found the same thing as Zacarías; there were too many people and hardly any jobs. Those were bitter times for all of us, confusing most of us, enraging others, especially since few could explain why such a thing was happening.

On the one side, voices said that it was a government thing, and that the greedy politicos were pulling strings to fill up their pockets. On the other side, people made bets that it was the gringos who were responsible because everyone knew how greedy they were and how little they respected us. Whatever was the reason, the truth was that we all sank deeper into poverty with each day.

Our family became gloomy and pessimistic when we were together, and the day came when we hardly spoke to one another. When we did come together, it was to complain

*or argue and shout at one another. It usually ended with one
of us crying or running off to another room; our house was
filled with the sound of shouting or a terrible silence.*

*Then the inevitable finally hit our family. One day
Zacarías let us know that he had decided to go to the United
States where he'd work to send us money to live. Now that I
think of it, I see that his mother and father weren't surprised.
I think they expected it to happen. As for me, I can say that
I wasn't surprised either, but I was hurt that he didn't talk to
me about what he was thinking or planning; he had kept his
intentions buried deep inside himself. I felt that he had treated me like an outsider, not the person who lived and slept
with him. I told him what I felt, but instead of coming to an
understanding we had a terrible argument and he went away
without speaking to me.*

*That day was the turning point in our life. I'm certain of
that now because less than three weeks later a man came to
tell me that Zacarías was in a hospital in Piedras Negras. He
had been badly injured when he fell while trying to jump on
a moving freight train. Without even packing a bag I took a
bus that night, and when I got off the bus I went to the hospital where I found Zacarías, or what was left of him.*

*To reach him I had to walk down a long dormitory littered
with cramped beds with here a boy missing an arm and over
there another with both feet sheared off. Everywhere I looked
there were men with missing limbs, some unconscious, others
delirious, yet others crying out for help. Some of the beds
were still bloodied because the victim had barely been dragged
away. The stink in the ward was so sickening that I had to
cover my mouth as I tried to keep from vomiting.*

*It didn't take long before I saw Zacarías; he had his eyes
closed, but I knew that he was conscious. At that moment I*

wished that he had been lost in another world, drugged or in a coma, because I saw that he had lost his legs above the knees. Only bandaged stumps of what used to be his thighs showed from below a hospital gown. When I got close to him, he opened his eyes, but he didn't speak.

I barely got to his side when I was told that he had to be released from the hospital because others were waiting for the bed, so we returned home before he regained strength and health. He was forced to use a wheelchair and he didn't resist it although I knew that he was in pain whenever I moved him in and out of it. He didn't complain even when I helped him relieve himself and change his clothing. To look at him broke my heart because I saw that he was alive, but his body was half of what it had been, and his soul was even more mutilated.

Time dragged during those terrible months, and after some time I found work in a big house that kept several maids. I was put in charge of cleaning toilets and scrubbing what seemed corridors without end, but because it paid money that helped our family, I was grateful. Everyday, when my tasks were finished, I hurried home to help tend to Adina and Zacarías, but those were unhappy times because I saw his frustration and depression grow deeper. I didn't know what to do to lessen his anguish, and because I didn't do anything, I think he saw this as indifference on my part. In time, a deep coldness crept in between us until we hardly spoke to one another.

Our relationship was more complicated than merely not speaking, and now I know that it was my fault that the distance between us became worse every day. I should say every night, because that was when Zacarías let me know that he desired intimacy with me. When he first spoke to me about it, I was confused because I had thought that we would never again take the same pleasure we used to have, and the truth is that I felt uneasy, even anxious when he spoke of it.

I don't know why, but I felt afraid when he asked me to submit to him. At first I pretended not to hear him, and I turned away in the bed to make him think that I was asleep. I did this a few times, but I didn't fool him because he became more obstinate. Each night he cried and begged while he tried to force me to let him get between my legs. When I resisted, it became a terrible battle between the two of us. He pulled, and I pushed. I scratched him, and he pummeled me, all the time terrible words spilled out of our clenched teeth. Our fight became a nightly struggle until I finally gave in.

It was a mistake because the sensation of his mutilated thighs between mine filled me with indescribable disgust. I couldn't help it. I tried to remember his once caressing legs, but too much had changed; what was left of him was a piece of what he had been. So instead of giving my body to Zacarías I struggled against his clinging arms. What used to be caresses and sighs turned into clumsy fumbling and groping. I know that I broke his heart, but I couldn't force myself to do what he desired and needed so much. My feelings were even more complicated by the poverty that was devouring our lives, filling me with bitterness and anger. I had to admit that I could no longer love him or anyone else.

After that our days went on as usual. I lived with only one thing in mind—to erase everything that was happening to us. I concentrated on what to do next, especially for Adina, who was growing. All I wanted was to shield my daughter from the unhappiness that was polluting our world and even more from the hunger that hounded us every day.

The River Flows North

My pay brought little food to our table, and all the time I watched my little girl growing thinner while my desperation grew.

The house where I worked was a grand one that seemed to float above the misery gripping the rest of us. The family had several grown children, each with a car and fine clothing; they were happy, loud, always shouting, laughing, playing jokes on one another and they entertained friends and family almost every day. Everywhere I looked I saw an abundance of everything. The kitchen overflowed with food and treats. Closets were crammed with the latest fashions and countless pairs of shoes. Their fingers, wrists and ears glittered with expensive jewelry. When I looked at them I became more envious and angry that some people had so much and the rest of us went to bed hungry.

Now I see that I allowed myself to become obsessed with that family's wealth. Above all, I became fixated on the kitchen that was always stuffed with so much food that the maids complained about it not fitting in the refrigerators and pantries, so I suppose that what came next was bound to happen. One day when I found the kitchen unattended, I helped myself to a chunk of meat. It was so easy. I just buried that treasure deep in the bag already stuffed with my apron and sweater. Nobody noticed or cared.

Afterward I did it almost every day, and it became easier each time. I found bringing food to my family a natural thing because there was so much of it in that rich kitchen and because it was there for the taking. I told myself that it was unfair that my little girl was shrinking down to her bones while food was going to waste elsewhere. Besides, those people didn't even notice.

My family knew what I was doing, but what were they to do? They understood and never questioned me. Instead we ate, silently grateful that we had at least one more meal to keep us. During those times no one looked into my eyes until the day one of the sons of my employer appeared at the door to tell everyone that I was a thief. He said that I was fired and that I would be arrested if I again went close to that big house.

When the man left us, no one said anything but I knew that they were feeling the same shame that was choking me. Without a word I got to my feet and went to the room I shared with Zacarías. I closed the door and laid on the bed where I stayed in darkness without moving or sleeping, ready to reject Zacarías when he tried to come to me. He didn't come. I was alone while my humiliation grew, and it became more intense with each moment until I felt my nerves shatter. My mind swirled. When had I taken the wrong path? When did my disgrace begin?

I had become a common thief. I had to face that shame, and the more I looked at that ugly truth, the deeper I slipped into sadness. I don't know how many days passed while I refused to leave the darkness of the room, because it was the only thing that protected me from what I thought were the accusing eyes of my family. I refused food and even water. I didn't want to speak to anyone, and, as time passed, I sank deeper into the mud of wretchedness.

I don't know what brought me back. Maybe it was that I sank so deep into that pit that I hit something hard, unbending, telling me that I had to come to my senses. First, I tried to convince myself that I had not had a choice, and I told myself that I was not different from others who were stealing to put food on their table. Oh, I gave myself many other reasons why I wasn't to blame, but in the end I saw it all meant nothing. I was a thief.

It was then that an idea began to take root. I thought of the men and women that went north to work for the gringos. Zacarías had been one of them, but he had been blocked not because he was a coward, but because something more powerful had stopped him. I pictured those people heading to bus stations and roads, ready to venture out to unknown places.

At first it was just a spark that got into my head, but the more I thought about it the more it grew. At times I told the noise in my head to keep quiet because what others were doing was not what I was able to do because I had never risked anything by myself. I hadn't even left my town except once or twice, and that was with my family. These thoughts scared me, but what choice did I have? I was the only one of our family able to work, and there was nothing where I lived to help feed us.

I got off the bed, bathed, dressed and went to where my family was huddled. I saw that they, too, were trying to find a way out of our poverty. When I walked into the room their faces turned toward me, and, although no one said anything, I saw in those expressions that they knew and accepted what was inevitable. Even Zacarías overcame the fire inside him when he told me to go, to be careful and to come back to them.

I made my way al norte like everyone else. I walked, hitched rides; now and then even a bus stopped to pick up a handful of us. I didn't have money but somehow along the way I got food and shelter. It didn't take long before I edged up to the small group that was listening to el coyote who called himself Leonardo Cerda. I paid attention as he laid out the plan to cross the desert into the United States, espe-

cially when he talked about work and the good money that was waiting for us.

When it was my turn to pay, I told him that I didn't have money and that I would pay him as soon as I found work on the other side, but he didn't like my proposition. I thought that he would tell me to go away, but he didn't. After he kicked his boot in the sand and scratched his head he said that he was willing to take me on one condition: That I agree to pay him somewhere along the crossing. Once would be enough, he said. Although I knew what he meant, I said yes.

FOURTEEN

Day Five

Night had ended when a dry hiss in Celia's throat shook Menda out of the stupor into which she had fallen, and in the dim light she managed to see that Borrego was sprawled out next to her. A few moments passed before she crawled over to Celia, but by the time she reached her the rattle had stopped. When she took the woman in her arms, she realized that she was dead. Sitting on her haunches, Menda took hold of the body and held Celia close to her, rocking back and forth while tears rolled down her face. She gently stroked Celia's forehead and cheeks as if the touch of her hand might bring her back. Then, without warning, the silhouette of the battered van flashed in Menda's mind, evoking images of twisted, dried out corpses.

"*¡Dios mío!*"

Menda first whispered, but then uttered those words in a loud voice until she shouted them over and again as her voice soared, shrill with anguish. She didn't try to hold back her cries because she couldn't. She wept for Celia, but also for herself and for the rest of their lost group. One by one they had disappeared into the mysterious desert sands, and now only she and Borrego were left, so Menda sobbed from fear and grief. Cradling Celia's body, Menda grieved. Her wailing became louder and so intense that her forlorn lament shook Borrego out of unconsciousness.

When he sat up, one look told him what was happening. He slithered over to console her because he hoped to calm her, but nothing he did stopped Menda from crying. He tried to take Celia's body from her, but her arms were latched on tight to the corpse. In distress, he wrapped his arms around both of them, while he begged Menda to please stop crying. He tried to remind her that Celia was at rest and free from the horror they still faced. Whatever Borrego said was useless because the howls went on and on.

Then he took hold of Menda's face and pressed his forehead against hers, but when he brought her face closer, his eyes suddenly became fixated on her moistened cheeks. He tried to look away from her tears, but he couldn't help himself because now his eyes were riveted on the rows etched on her cheeks by those fat watery blobs. His fevered mind slipped, and he imagined that they were miniature canals that carried sparkling water from the brim of her eyes down to her chin. The more Borrego stared at her face, the more Menda's tears became fresh streams of water, and he found it impossible to look away because all he could think of was that his tongue clung to the roof of his mouth, desperate to escape its thirst.

The River Flows North

Borrego stuck out his parched tongue and started licking Menda's face like a thirst-crazed dog, and he did it so rapidly and with such frenzy that it took her a few seconds to snap out of her grief to realize what he was doing. When that happened she let go of Celia's body and lashed out at him with both hands. She banged him on the chest with so much fury that she sent him rolling on his back. At the same time she screamed out, "What are you doing? Have you gone crazy?"

Flat on his butt and stunned, Borrego stared at Menda. He didn't know what to say because he couldn't explain what had gotten into him. "I don't know. I don't know. *¡Dios mío!* Yes! I'm going crazy. I don't know what made me do that, Menda. I'm sorry. Please forgive me."

She looked at him for a long time, but slowly her expression changed from anger to sadness, and her body let go of the tension that had filled it when she struck him. Then she turned her attention to Celia's body as she slid it off her lap, gingerly laid it on its back and made sure that its eyes were shut. She got on her knees, made the sign of the cross, and gestured for Borrego to come closer. "Borrego, come, let's pray for Celia's soul. Maybe that will keep us from going crazy."

The two then joined to pray, but all they could do was mumble incoherently because no matter how much each tried, neither could remember the words of even one Hail Mary. Too exhausted to stay on their knees, they slouched over the body and they cried like lost children. In a few minutes Menda dug at the sand with her hands, clawing away with useless, sloppy strokes that barely made a dent. Borrego saw what she was doing so he, too, burrowed as hard as he could.

The two hollowed out a shallow pit where they slipped in Celia's body. After that they shoved as much sand as they could to cover the body along with a few stones they gathered. Finally Borrego twisted twigs into a tiny cross that he stuck on top of the mound. With what strength they had left, Menda and Borrego staggered away from Celia's burial place. They dragged themselves as they tried to keep the mountains on their right side.

It was still morning, but it was already intolerably hot. The rags that covered them weren't enough to cover their bodies against the sun that burned them painfully, but it was their scalps that were hurting the most, so they struggled with whatever material might cover at least a part of their heads. Borrego yanked off what was left of his shirt and tied it like a turban around his head, but the only garment still left on Menda was her bra. Like Borrego she ripped it off to lash it around her head. This left them nearly naked and exposed from the waist up to their necks, but neither was ashamed of their nakedness because they felt only the pain of burning skin.

They lost track of time, and although the head cover had given them enough relief to stagger forward, neither could tell if hours or minutes had gone by, but, as time passed, thirst more and more overwhelmed their thinking. Their thoughts twisted in and out of coherence until they instinctively knew that they could not go farther. When that happened they collapsed by the side of a clump of saguaros where they crawled as close as they could to the skimpy shade, and there they huddled. They crouched panting in a stupor as they gawked at each other, barely recognizing the face that peered back. Traumatized, each one rolled over on the sand and surrendered to fatigue until Borrego half whispered, "We're going to die, Menda."

She struggled onto her elbow, trying to face him. "No! We're going to live! There has to be a reason for all of this misery. It can't be for nothing. We're going to live, Borrego. I promise you."

"You're wrong. I'm going to die just like my brother."

"How do you know your brother's not alive?"

Borrego glared at Menda because he could not believe her words; he was convinced that Nicanor had perished. "There's not a chance that he's alive, so stop talking that way. If you're trying to keep up my hopes, stop it. It hurts more than admitting that he's dead."

Menda saw the anguish in Borrego's face so she kept quiet and slumped back on the sand, eyes closed. After a while it occurred to her that maybe if they found something to dig at the spiky saguaro's skin, they might be able to suck out at least a few drops of moisture. She stuck her hands in the pockets of her pants, but it was useless; they were in tatters. She propped herself up, scanned the sand close to where they were sprawled, and she caught sight of a small stone that had a sharp edge. She snatched it up as if it was about to run away from her.

"Borrego, look!"

"What?"

"Let's scratch the saguaro. Maybe there's something we can suck."

He took the rock and tried to cut into the thick bark, but he was so weak that he barely scratched the prickly skin. He tried again, this time with more force until he was able to cut into the surface. He did it again and again until a few drops of sap oozed out. The sight of the liquid thrilled them so much that they let out a yelp, but it was a weak, guttural croak that sounded as if it had come from the pit of their stomachs. In seconds, they anxiously took turns as they sucked, but each draw left their mouths wounded by sharp needles that defended the saguaro against their invasive lips. The cactus gave up little moisture, but it was something, enough to give Menda and Borrego more time.

The sun dipped toward the west, and the heat backed down. Soon night with its bitter cold would assault them again. Menda moved. First she slithered on her belly, then after a few feet she got on her hands and knees until she was able to hoist herself erect. She swayed unsteadily for a few seconds, but then she got her balance, and when she felt sure of herself she turned to Borrego.

"Come, Borrego! We still have some daylight. Let's keep moving."

"What for? We're dead. I'm staying here by this *pinche* saguaro. At least here I feel like somebody's watching over me. You go, Menda. I can't move anymore."

She did not pay attention to him. Instead she staggered back to where he was crouched, put her hands under his armpits and tried to yank him onto his feet, but she was so weak that all she did was make him wobble from one side to the other. Still, Menda would not give up, so she then grabbed fistfuls of Borrego's hair and pulled. It was such an effort for her that she let out a grunt each time she yanked, but it worked because pain forced him to get to his feet. He scowled at her.

She glared back at him. "I don't care if you want to die. I'm not going to leave you here. We're moving together or nothing. We're almost there, I tell you," Menda's voice was hoarse so she could only whisper, but he understood what she said.

"¡Loca!" Borrego hurled the insult with as much force as he could summon. "You don't know what you're talking about. Can't you see we're finished?"

"Look, Borrego, you might be right, but maybe you're wrong. We can still move, can't we?" When he nodded his head, Menda went on. "Well then, let's move!"

"What makes you think that we're going to make it?"

"Doña Encarnación."

"What? Menda, the old lady's gone. Dead! Buried somewhere under all this devil sand! If you still think she's going to get us out of this trap it proves you're crazy!"

"¡Sí! She's dead, but still with us. I feel her. Sometimes I see her."

"You *are* crazy!"

"I don't care what you think, Borrego. Just come with me!" Menda mumbled her words while she took hold of one of Borrego's arms, wrapped it over her shoulders and, nearly dragging him, she moved forward little by little, step by step, even as their feet sank deeper into the sand. After a while Borrego saw something in the distance, and the sight somehow gave him new energy. He whipped his arm away from Menda as he lunged headlong tripping and stumbling. She squinted and tried to make out what he saw.

"Look! It's my brother! Nicanor is sitting under that little tree!"

Borrego's voice cracked with the stress of emotion. He pointed his shaky hand as he pitched forward and tried to run. All along he shouted although his voice hardly had any volume. "Nicanor! *¡Hermano!* We're here! We're here! You're safe!"

Menda stopped where she was because now she, too, made out the figure of a man that appeared to be sitting under a tree, but she saw that there was something wrong with the man's posture. Something was off with the way his head slumped over his chest, and what was most off was that the man's rump did not touch the surface of the sand. He was hanging, not sitting, even her blurred vision could tell that much. In a moment she understood.

"Borrego! *¡Por Dios!* Stop!"

Her shout went unheard because Borrego had already lunged toward the body without focusing on what waited. He staggered, fell, then picked himself up only to stumble again as he plunged headlong toward his brother, yelling and wildly flapping his arms. Menda tried to catch up with Borrego, but it was useless because she was too heavy. Her legs felt like posts that sank deeper into the sand with each step. When she saw Borrego reach the man, she gave up and slumped onto her knees while she covered her eyes.

She waited for the scream, but there was none. After a few seconds she dropped her hands from her eyes to see what happened. She saw that Borrego now held his brother in his arms and that he struggled with the belt that bound Nicanor's neck to a branch of an ironwood tree, so stunted that the only way for anyone to hang himself would be to sit and pull. By the time Menda reached Borrego he was trying to loosen the buckle that was lodged under his brother's chin, but no matter how much he struggled, his fingers were too swollen to pry it loose.

Menda moved Borrego's hands aside while she said, "Help me lift him." With that small slack, she was able to force her fingers around the buckle until it came apart. Once loosened from the belt, the body's head wobbled from side to side, so Borrego tried to steady his brother's head by taking him in his arms, and, for a long time, he rocked the body while he cried. Borrego mumbled words that Menda could not make out, but she knew they were expressions of love mixed with prayers, and even curses. She got as close as she could to him and ran her hands over Borrego's head. She did not know another way to let him know how sorry she was that his brother had chosen to take his life in such a painful way.

"Borrego, he's not suffering anymore."

"¡Dios Santo! Why didn't he wait for me?"

"I don't know. He was called and he answered. He's with the rest of them now. Have faith, Borrego. Remember, he's not alone. He's with Celia and Doña Encarnación." Then she added, "And the others we left behind in the van."

Menda put her face close to Borrego's. She knew that he was looking intensely at her, that he tried to believe what she said, but she did not say anymore. Instead she wept, and her cries came from a depth that surprised her because she had not realized that she could feel such tenderness for someone she barely knew. She did not try to hold back her tears. She cried for Borrego, for his brother and for their family. She grieved for the others and for herself. Her heart ached for all the nameless people that had perished in that wasteland, who would never live to reach the land that had filled their heads with dreams.

Night had fallen, and its darkness wrapped itself around Borrego and Menda. They knew that they had to bury Nicanor, but they were too exhausted to do it, and the dark made it impossible for them to see what they were doing. So they stretched out the body, folded its arms on its chest and prepared to keep vigil just as if Nicanor had been laid out in

157

a coffin in his home, surrounded by parents and family that mourned.

Menda and Borrego, like guardian angels, sat on either side of the body. They said nothing, but understood everything. After a while she came around to Borrego and tried to take him in her arms because she knew that he needed consolation, but when she pressed him close she flinched, suddenly aware of unbearable pain. In the anxiety over the discovery of Nicanor she had not realized that her breasts, arms and shoulders were blistered raw from exposure, so without thinking, she pushed him away. Then she remembered that Borrego's skin was just as injured, so again she moved close to him, but this time she took his hands in hers. After a while she stroked his forehead as she would have done had her own son been in anguish. Borrego leaned toward her, letting her know that he understood what her fingers said to him. After a while she whispered, "Let's keep your brother company while he finds his way to the others."

Night crept over them while they kept watch. As the hours passed, Menda listened to the murmurs and sighs that filtered from beneath the sand, and Borrego surrendered to memories of his and Nicanor's life.

FIFTEEN

Borrego and Nicanor Osuna

*T*he first time we tried to cross the border, la Migra
caught us and threw us out, but we waited a while
on the other side and tried again, this time through
the desert. People might wonder what made us try
again, even in the face of humiliations, hunger, anger, and
stupid decisions, but no one stops to think that what we left
behind was even worse.

My brother and I did it together because we were always
together. We hardly ever fought or disagreed; we saw everything as if we had only one pair of eyes between the both of
us. Ever since we were boys we acted like one, sometimes we
got confused, forgetting who was Borrego and who was
Nicanor. People always thought that we were twins, and, to
tell the truth, I think we should have been twins since we
were so much alike.

Nicanor was older by less than a year, but, because I grew a little bit faster, we were almost the same size from when we were still boys. We looked alike, too, except I had tight curly hair that stuck out around my head, and Nicanor had straight hair. As we grew we became closer and closer, and we almost always did the same thing at the same time, like reflections in a mirror. Anyone who knew us called us sombras because we moved and walked like shadows of one another.

We were born in Zacatecas on the outskirts of a small town called Tecolotes. Our father and mother lived on a ranchito they rented from a patrón; there they planted and harvested maíz. My brother and I were born on that land, and we grew there until a few years ago when the harvest dried up on us.

After Nicanor and I were born, two little sisters came along. Their names are Evita and Nereyda, but because they were much younger I don't remember growing up with them. I think my mother had other kids besides the four of us because there's a big space between the girls and me, but I don't know for sure because I never asked.

My mother and father were humble people with roots deep in the dirt. They always wanted to own their rancho, but the years passed and they never got enough money, so there was nothing else but to work somebody else's land and pay rent. This went on for years until one year the worst happened. The water that irrigated our maíz field plugged up, or changed its direction, or something like that, and, without water, the crop dried up so fast that we didn't even have a chance to harvest at least some of the corn.

The River Flows North

Apá went to el patrón hoping to get help, but when he understood that el patrón knew about our crop failure, that what happened with the water shortage was part of a bigger plan, apá got very angry. My brother and I were there, and we saw what happened when our father lost control of himself. It started with harsh, bad words, then screaming and pushing, and soon fists and kicking took both men down to the ground where blood flowed. Apá won the fight, but lost the rancho, and that meant that we had to get off the property. Later on we found out that el patrón had sold the land to a tomato harvesting company, and he did it without telling us or giving us time to look for a different way of life.

That was the beginning of hard times for our family. Our parents were forced to work picking those pinche tomatoes. Nicanor and I did the same thing, but no matter how many hours we worked, we couldn't put together enough money to get a little house for the six of us so we had to go live with one of amá's sisters. We worked our asses off stooped over tomato plants from when the sun came out to when it disappeared, and we hardly got enough to put tortillas and beans on the table.

The day came when Nicanor and I knew we had to do more to help out our family, so we decided to move over to the little town called Tecolotes to look for work there. We were lucky because we found a job at a mill that ground and mixed up maíz, making it ready for people to make tortillas. All day long we shoveled the dough into a big grinder. It was hard work, but it paid more than picking tomatoes, so we were grateful. Then that work dried up, too, although it didn't happen suddenly; it happened over months, little by little, until the machines were turned off. It's hard to believe, but the whole thing happened because of a stinking two-kilo paper sack.

In the beginning nobody at the mill knew what or why it happened except that fewer people came to buy dough. We didn't notice it right away, but after a while we saw that at the end of the day there were kilos of dough left over although we ground up the same amount of maíz. We tried to explain it. Was it that people didn't eat tortillas anymore? Impossible! Who ever heard of anyone living without tortillas? And it got worse with each month until the owner finally came to say that the mill had closed down, and he told us the reason.

A new product had come into stores, a dough in powdered form that turned into the real thing when mixed with a little bit of water. When that was done, anyone could put together a pile of delicious tortillas. Even more important, people saved money because that little two-kilo sack made more dough for less money than what people paid at the mill. What was better, everyone said, was that now no one had to walk to the mill, stand in line to buy the dough and then lug it back to the kitchen to put those tortillas on the hot stove. What excited everyone, especially women, was that this new thing could be whipped up any time of day.

A shitty two-kilo paper sack took away our jobs. Oh, I don't mean that it happened overnight, because it didn't. It took time, but when it happened, it hit everybody. Just like that, the door shut down on us, and now we didn't have a job, nothing to help our family. After that, Nicanor and I moved out to neighboring towns, hoping to find some kind of a job, but it was useless because everywhere we looked there were at least fifty people waiting in line in front of us.

The River Flows North

Now we felt the same desperation other people were feeling, especially when we saw that our little sisters went hungry. We talked about it, sometimes all night long, but no matter how much we looked for a way out we just couldn't think of what to do. What we saw more and more were people making their way al norte, and it happened every day, so in time we decided to do the same thing. The problem was that we knew that once anyone reached the border, a guide was needed, and we knew, too, that most coyotes charged at least a thousand American dollars for each person. Hearing that big number almost made us lose courage, but after a few days of thinking and talking, Nicanor and I decided that we had to do it. The important thing was to make our way to the border; after that something would come up for sure.

We didn't know exactly which way to take, but it didn't matter because most of the main roads in Mexico point in this direction. We hitched rides, jumped on the back of buses, climbed on the roofs of cargo trains—just to cut across Mexico: first up through Durango and then over to Chihuahua and Sonora until we made it to Baja. Many times we even walked, but we didn't care because we knew that all we had to do was cross the fence that said on this side is Mexico and over there is the United States. After that our dream would begin. We were sure of it.

What was our dream? As we walked roads and crouched in trains, the only thing Nicanor and I talked about was what we were going to do once we got to the other side. We're campesinos, and the earth is where we wanted to plant our roots, so what we dreamed about was to work on a farm for maybe eight or ten years while we saved our money. We would look around until we found what we wanted, buy our

*land and then send for our family. This part of our dream
made us ask ourselves where we would plant our roots. We
had already heard that the ocean was the most beautiful
thing that God made, but we had never seen it, so that's
where we planned to set up our rancho. We decided that we
wanted our land to be high up, close to the ocean where we
would cultivate and irrigate our plants. That way, as we
worked, when we needed to straighten up every now and
then, we would look out to see the sun sparkle on the ocean.
That's what Nicanor and I talked about; that was our dream.*

*But it wasn't all dream and talk for us because we knew
that it wouldn't be easy, so we kept on the move until we
reached Tijuana. Once we got there, we asked where we
should go to jump the fence, and, without asking who we
were or where we came from, people pointed to a place
called Mesa Otay. We made it to Otay, but we were surprised
when we saw that there were hundreds of compañeros and
compañeras all moving around like they were lost. Most of
them looked sad and hungry, and a lot of them had kids
hanging onto them. It was noisy because most everybody
shouted and screamed, asked this, answered that, and they
did it all at once so nobody could hear anything. There were
people that sold food, water and blankets, things that travelers need to make a trip; there were even peddlers selling wire
cutters.*

*I don't know what my brother and I expected, but in our
mind it wasn't supposed to be that way. We walked around
for a while to catch on to what was happening and what we
were supposed to do to get over to the other side. When we
thought we knew what to do next, we started to mix in and*

we asked people to help us with a coyote. It was easy. We found out that those jackals are everywhere.

When we got close to one, we had a hard time making a deal because we didn't have money, but we finally negotiated to pay him after we got work on the other side and to help out with the women and children of the group. This deal wasn't as easy as it sounds. He told us he would find us and kill us if we didn't pay him right away. We knew that he meant it.

Next day at dawn we all started the trip across the wire fence. We followed trampled pathways and even crept through big pipes filled up to our ankles with human shit. Those were the times that my brother and I helped out carrying kids and even pulling women who kept falling. We walked all day and stopped only for short rests to eat. Afterward we climbed hills, some of them high and rough. I was alert all the time because I expected la Migra to jump us any minute, but nothing happened. More and more I thought that el coyote really knew what he was doing because where he put his foot, there for sure was the right path.

When nighttime finally came, all of us were so beat up that we wanted to stop, but el coyote passed the word that since there was a moon with plenty of light we would keep on the move just a little bit more. It was hard on all of us, most of all on the kids who cried, but we kept it up until finally we came to a hill where we could rest, but I was too curious to keep still. I wanted to see what was on the other side, so I walked a little more, and there I saw it.

I waved to Nicanor to come see the most beautiful picture anyone alive has ever seen. Together we looked out over the ridge of the hill down on a city of lights that sparkled in the distance like millions of stars, and just on the other side of that immense city was a flat sheet of silver that reflected the moon like a mirror. We threw our arms around each other and cried because our dream wasn't a dream. The land by the ocean really existed, and our eyes were looking at it.

We were so happy that we lost track of what was happening, but then we heard el coyote's whisper. ¡Abajo, pendejos! ¡Allí viene la Migra! We flopped on our bellies and hardly breathed. Our ears got stiff and stuck up in the air like dogs that sense the intruder, but we didn't hear anything, just the bushes that moved in the wind. I almost laughed because I thought that the guy was so stupid that the rustle of the bushes made him think that it was la Migra, but before I could poke Nicanor with my elbow, a big light clicked on, pinning all of us to the ground. I felt that the lamp's blue rays were spikes of steel, and I froze, stretched out flat on my belly, eyes closed. When I opened them, I saw that everybody shook like wet animals, and nobody moved because we were paralyzed with fear. The worst had happened.

Then a vehicle came from I don't know where; soon tall men in uniforms packed all of us into it. The doors slammed behind us, and when we felt the truck move, we looked at one another without knowing what to say; some of us cried. After a while I looked around for el coyote but I saw that he had escaped. He disappeared with everybody's money, and the only thing those people could do was to curse him and his mother. In a few hours, the truck covered the distance that took us a whole day to walk, and when those big back doors opened, we were shoved back into Mexico. Later on we found out that we were lucky because if we had been trapped deeper in California we would have landed in jail.

The River Flows North

My brother and I disappeared into the streets of Tijuana, where we drifted, scared by so many people, and so much noise. Some of them looked lost, just like us, but most of them were pissed and mean looking. Everywhere there were curses and shouts, but even more fights. We were afraid, and everything we saw told us to go back home, but we couldn't because we had caught a look at what we came for. How could we go back now that we were so close to that place by the ocean? We couldn't stop thinking that if we got that near once, then we could do it again. So we wandered in and out of those streets although we didn't know what to do.

What happened next is shameful. I did something that I never imagined I could do, yet I did it. Not too many days passed when a man dressed in a fancy suit got near us and started a conversation. We didn't know anybody so we were surprised, but when he tapped me on the shoulder, he did it like he knew me, so I listened to what he had to say. He didn't lose time. He had work for us, he said, so we got interested right away, that is, until he told us what it was all about. He said that he had clients that were rich men and liked a little action with good-looking boys like us. The work? All there was to it was doing like we were told. The pay? More money in one month than a couple of years bent over rows of plants. That was it. It would be easy, he said.

At first I stared at the man because I thought that I didn't understand him, but in a minute I understood. I'm a campesino, but I'm not stupid. I knew what the stranger was offering us. I suppose that because it was so shameful I couldn't believe that it was happening to us. I turned and walked away, certain that my brother was behind me.

Nicanor and I walked for a long time until I knew that we had to talk because I needed to know what was going on in his head. When I looked at him, his face was like a mask, and his expression didn't change for a long time until he finally opened up. Nicanor said that it was our only way out, that it didn't matter if we did whatever the stranger wanted, it would be our secret, and no one would ever know. The important thing, he said, was to remember that doing it would get us the money we needed, and we could forget it as soon as we made our way to the other side of the border.

I listened to Nicanor although I couldn't believe my ears were hearing what he was saying. I was more shocked by his words than by the strangers proposition. Then I told him that I couldn't do it no matter how we thought of it, or talked about it. I talked and talked saying that I could never forget doing such a thing and that I preferred to work bent over plants all my life, even starve to death before I did those dirty things. He looked at me for a long time without saying anything, but his eyes were cold and different. Then he turned his back and walked away, but when I saw him leaving me, it hurt so much that I changed my mind. The whole thing happened fast; without thinking I followed and told him that I would do it. Blame me! That was all Nicanor said, and we never again spoke about that terrible day.

It was easy to find the stranger because he was standing at the same street corner as before, and he had a big smile on his face when he gave us money to buy clothes, cut our hair and get a bath. I felt ashamed when I saw that he knew that we would return, and, even without asking our names, he gave us instructions of where and at what time to find him that night.

The River Flows North

After we agreed to everything the man told us to do, the meetings with different men started and went on for months. We did it with those strangers until we got enough money to make the crossing, but all the time never forgot that what we were doing was bad. We sold ourselves. We didn't talk about it. We just pretended that it wasn't happening, but I knew that Nicanor felt just as dirty as I did.

I know now that he killed himself because he was too ashamed to keep on living, and I know, too, that he felt guilty because he thought he got me to let those men do those things to me. I never told him that he didn't have to convince me to do it. I never told him that I made up my own mind; nobody forced me. Now he's dead, and it's only me left alive to feel the shame.

SIXTEEN

The Last Day

Menda moved closer to Borrego when she saw him sway from side to side; she knew that he was about to faint even though his body was upright. On an impulse, she glanced down at Nicanor's corpse, and deep regret again overcame her because of his shame, but most of all because he took his life when he had almost reached his dream.

Menda wanted to bury him, but she knew that neither she nor Borrego had the strength to dig even a shallow pit. The only thing she could think of doing was to scratch off pieces of the body's shirt to cover its face. On top of that she piled sand and patted it down while she whispered whatever prayers she could conjure. When she finished, she slung one of Borrego's arms over her shoulders and struggled to her feet.

"C'mon, Borrego!"

The River Flows North

"No! I can't leave my brother!"

"You're coming with me. Your brother isn't here anymore. He's over there. See where I'm pointing? Open your eyes! Look, there, where the sand becomes a hill. That's where he's waiting for us. He's standing there with Celia and Doña Encarnación."

Menda pointed with a shaky finger toward what appeared to be an embankment that rose from the sand, although she was uncertain of what she saw because the sun was already playing its tricks of light and shadows. Suddenly she looked down and stared for a long time because her blurred vision almost convinced her that it was not sand that was swirling around her ankles; it was cool splashing water enticing her to plunge into it. Frightened by what she thought she saw, Menda forced herself to look up as she pushed harder to drag Borrego along each step.

"Borrego, come!"

Only a few yards separated them from the embankment, a distance ordinarily covered in minutes, but it took Menda nearly an hour to drag herself and Borrego to that point. They staggered, fell, struggled to their feet only to fall again countless times, and all the while it was Menda who pushed and pulled until they reached the incline. The embankment was only a few feet high, but because they did not have the strength to climb it they collapsed at its base.

Menda fainted. When she awoke she could not tell how long she had been unconscious; what she did know was that she held Borrego in a tight grip. Her arms were wrapped around him, but he was so still she thought he had died. She shook him and tapped his face hoping for a response, but there was nothing. The only thing that let her know that he was still alive was a slight flutter of his eyelids.

Without letting go of him she looked around, then up and down until she saw that they were sprawled against the embankment she had thought was a mirage. It took her a few seconds to realize that it was real, that she was not hallucinating, that they had reached the edge of the desert. It was in that instant that she thought she heard the faint drone of a car, so she listened, ears keen and alert, wanting to hear more. Her eyes widened as if they, too, could hear.

After a few seconds she let go of Borrego and crawled up to the edge of the incline. When she reached it, like a frightened animal, she slowly raised her head inch by inch. First the tips of her stiffened hair cleared the top of the mound, then her forehead, until her eyes were level with the flat ground. Stretched out in front of her was a black strip of asphalt. It was a road.

"¡Borrego, *la Ocho! ¡Es la Ocho!*"

Menda's voice was a dry croak, and although she knew that Borrego could not hear her, she was crying so hard that she could not try again. Minutes passed while she wept, laughed and then cried again. She no longer felt the pain of her blistered flesh, of her tormented stomach and her parched swollen tongue. What she did feel was indescribable gratitude that she and Borrego had lived to see the flat black hardness of a road that would lead them out of that desolation.

She scrambled down to Borrego. She did not care that she tumbled and rolled headlong and that she did not feel anything except the intense desire to get to her companion, to haul him up to the side of the road where surely a passing car would stop to help them. When she reached him, Borrego had begun to stir. Evidently her cracked voice had roused him, and he lifted his arms to cling to her. Together, very slowly, they slithered up the incline to the top where, too exhausted to do more, they collapsed on the side of the road.

Borrego mumbled and gasped for air before he lost consciousness again despite Menda's efforts to keep him awake. She was afraid that he would die so she shook his shoulders and slapped his face, and she did it even harder when she saw his eyes rolling back in their sockets. In a while he blinked and struggled to regain consciousness.

"Borrego, listen to me. Think of the place by the ocean! Live, Borrego! Stay alive! You'll see, a car will come, and someone will help us."

Menda tried desperately to keep Borrego alive with her words; she thought she was speaking to him, but her voice could not be heard; extreme thirst had pasted her tongue to the roof of her mouth. Her mind soon began to drift away to another world, to another time when she was a child, and when she grew to be a woman. Cloudy thoughts plucked her from the desert; they carried her to the green mountains of Chalatenango, to the waters of el Río Sumpul.

Menda was jolted back to consciousness when she heard voices. At first they were faint, but as the talk went on its echo grew stronger. She tried to open her eyes because she thought that it would help her make out what she heard, but it was impossible to open them because her eyelids had by now fused shut. Gradually she made out two voices, but, although they neared, their words still did not take shape. She listened carefully, and by the time her ears focused, she realized that those tongues spoke a language unknown to her. This frightened her so much that when the first voice came close to her she held Borrego against her body with even more force.

"Christ! Look at them! They look like hamburger."

"I've seen worse."

"You're kidding! Looks like they've been chewed up by coyotes."

"I'm telling you, I've seen worse. Get to the truck and bring some blankets and water. Quick! Move!"

¡Inglés! Menda realized that what the faceless voices spoke was English, the language of the United States, and, although she did not understand what they said, she knew that she and Borrego had reached *la Ocho*. She felt fat tears spring from behind her eyeballs as they made their way to squeeze out from under her clamped lids.

"Look! I think she's crying!"

"Yeah! She's alive, all right. Come on! Let's give them some water. Just a little at a time. Too much will kill them for sure. There, just see how they're lapping it up."

The voices faded while Menda felt the trickle of water smear her lips as it made its way into her mouth, and from there down her throat which was shut tight, but in seconds it opened up. She felt wetness slip down into her stomach, and her mouth opened and shut begging for more. At the same time she felt Borrego move as he, too, drank, but still she would not let go of him.

"Help me pry her arms away from the kid so we can wrap each one up."

When Menda felt hands trying to pull her arms from Borrego, she resisted even though it took up the last of her strength; nothing was going to rip him away. In that moment of anxiety, she forced her eyes to look, but when her lids snapped open all she could make out were blurs that hung over her. She peered at two white blotches, round disks aimed at her, and it was not until the blurs spoke that she understood that they were faces.

"Shit! She ain't gonna let go of the kid!"

"Nope! Well, that's okay. Let's wrap them up together and put them in the truck. We can lift them between the two of us. C'mon! We'll throw a U-turn back to Ligurta."

"Ligurta? Why not go on to Gila Bend? We're already heading in that direction."

"Too far away, and they might not make it. Ligurta has a clinic. We can drop them off there."

"But we're already heading east. Hell! It's useless! Just look at them!"

"Goddammit! I tell you I've seen worse! They'll make it if we get them help quick."

"They're half dead already."

"Stop arguing, and help me haul them over to the truck."

Menda became aware of being lifted while she heard grunts and mutterings. At one point, when she and Borrego were almost dropped, she caught a string of barking words, and although she did not understand their meaning, she knew they were curses. In minutes, she and Borrego were carried deep into the rear of a truck where what she thought were folded blankets were put under their head, then she again tasted water when the rim of a bottle was placed to her lips. When more blankets were tucked around her the voices moved away; she heard the motor crank on, and then there was movement. All the while her arms never let go of Borrego.

As the vehicle picked up speed, Menda's body began to relax despite the pain that thrashed it; she lifted her head, trying to focus her eyes on what was around her. She first made out paneled sidings covered by canvas as well as the top of the cabin. Then she looked toward the open tail end of the truck, and she watched the road slip away, its dividing line was a white snake that slithered in the opposite direction with incredible speed. Above the moving road, there was blue sky telling her that night had turned to morning. Now she made out the sun just above the ridge of the mountains, the ones that had tricked her companions so many times, sometimes showing themselves, at other times hiding.

The hum of the truck's engine again transported Menda's thoughts back to Chalatenango, to her children and to all the others who had been a part of her life. Even Jacinto's blurred image appeared, but then quickly disappeared. She shut her inflamed eyes and hoped to doze off, but vivid images appeared behind her eyelids almost immediately. One by one her *compañeros* reappeared just as alive as they had been on that distant autumn morning when they stood around Leonardo Cerda. That picture then fused into the first night of the trek when they danced around the campfire.

From far away, faint harmonica music made its way to the rumbling truck where Menda held Borrego in a tight embrace. She heard Nicanor's music grow louder, stronger and she saw her *compañeros* again dance around the fire. Over there was Borrego, clowning around, swinging his butt back and forth as he invited everyone to join him. Soon, they were all at it. Celia, with arms stretched above her head, swayed to the music, and Menda saw herself dancing in her favorite *cumbia* way. And close by were Don Julio and Doña Encarnación as they moved slowly to the enticing sounds of Nicanor's harmonica. Even Manuelito shook his shoulders as he spun to the music's beat. The liveliest of them all was Leonardo Cerda, *el coyote,* who jiggled his skinny legs in the air while a cigarette dangled from his toothless gums. And as it happened that night, only Armando Guerrero stayed apart.

The River Flows North

As she swayed to the truck's motion, Menda looked hard at the images etched behind her closed eyelids. Her *compañeros* danced and whirled while the campfire cast their sharp silhouettes on the white sand of that forlorn desert. Suddenly, the illusion disappeared, and Menda's eyes snapped open to stare again at the road. She thought she saw Doña Encarnación standing by the side of the road. It receded until it became a tiny dot that evaporated into the desert air. After that, Menda closed her eyes and drifted back into unconsciousness.

ABOUT THE AUTHOR

Graciela Limón is the critically acclaimed and award-winning author of *Left Alive* (2005), *Erased Faces* (2001), *The Day of the Moon* (1999), *Song of the Hummingbird* (1996), *The Memories of Ana Calderón* (1994) and *In Search of Bernabé* (1993), the recipient of an American Book Award. Limón is Professor Emerita of Loyola Marymount University in Los Angeles, where she served as a professor of U.S. Latina/o Literature.

Books by Graciela Limón

La canción del colibrí

The Day of the Moon

El Día de la Luna

En busca de Bernabé

Erased Faces

In Search of Bernabé

Left Alive

The Memories of Ana Calderón

Song of the Hummingbird